Thomas the Obscure

Thomas
the Obscure

Maurice Blanchot

Translated by Robert Lamberton

Station Hill Press

Originally a French text published as *Thomas l'obscur* in Paris, France.
Copyright © 1941 by Editions Gallimard.

Published by Station Hill Press, Barrytown, New York 12507, with partial
financial support from the National Endowment for the Arts, a federal
agency in Washington D.C., and the New York State Council on the Arts.

Produced by the Institute for Publishing Arts, Barrytown, New York
12507, a not-for-profit, tax-exempt, organization.

Cover designed by Susan Quasha and George Quasha.

Library of Congress Cataloging-in-Publication Data

Blanchot, Maurice.
    [Thomas l'obscur. English]
    Thomas the obscure / by Maurice Blanchot. —New version /
translated by Robert Lamberton.
    p.   cm.
    Translation of: Thomas l'obscur.
    ISBN 0-88268-077-3   ISBN 0-88268-076-5 (pbk.)
    I. Title.
PQ2603.L3343T513   1988   88-20051
843'.912--dc19   CIP

Manufactured in the United States of America.

There is, for every work, an infinity of possible variants. The present version adds nothing to the pages entitled Thomas the Obscure begun in 1932, delivered to the publisher in May of 1940 and published in 1941, but as it subtracts a good deal from them, it may be said to be another, and even an entirely new version, but identical at the same time, if one is right in making no distinction between the figure and that which is, or believes itself to be, its center, whenever the complete figure itself expresses no more than the search for an imagined center.

Thomas the Obscure

I

THOMAS SAT DOWN and looked at the sea. He remained motionless for a time, as if he had come there to follow the movements of the other swimmers and, although the fog prevented him from seeing very far, he stayed there, obstinately, his eyes fixed on the bodies floating with difficulty. Then, when a more powerful wave reached him, he went down onto the sloping sand and slipped among the currents, which quickly immersed him. The sea was calm, and Thomas was in the habit of swimming for long periods without tiring. But today he had chosen a new route. The fog hid the shore. A cloud had come down upon the sea and the surface was lost in a glow which seemed the only truly real thing. Currents shook him, though without giving him the feeling of being in the midst of the waves and of rolling in familiar elements. The conviction that there was, in fact, no water at all made even his effort to swim into a frivolous exercise from which he drew nothing but discouragement. Perhaps he should only have had to get control of himself to drive away such thoughts, but his eye found nothing to cling to, and it seemed to him that he was staring into the void with the intention of finding help there. It was then that the sea, driven by the wind, broke loose. The storm tossed it, scattered it into inaccessible regions; the squalls turned the sky upside down and, at the same time, there reigned a silence and a calm which gave the impression that everything was already destroyed. Thomas sought to free himself from the insipid flood which was invading him. A piercing cold paralyzed his arms. The water swirled in whirlpools. Was it actually water? One moment the foam leapt before his eyes in whitish flakes, the next the absence of water took hold of his body and drew it along violently. His breathing became slower; for a few moments he held in his mouth

7

the liquid which the squalls drove against his head: a tepid
sweetness, strange brew of a man deprived of the sense of taste.
Then, whether from fatigue or for an unknown reason, his
limbs gave him the same sense of foreignness as the water in
which they were tossed. This feeling seemed almost pleasant at
first. As he swam, he pursued a sort of revery in which he confused himself with the sea. The intoxication of leaving himself,
of slipping into the void, of dispersing himself in the thought of
water, made him forget every discomfort. And even when this
ideal sea which he was becoming ever more intimately had in
turn become the real sea, in which he was virtually drowned, he
was not moved as he should have been: of course, there was
something intolerable about swimming this way, aimlessly,
with a body which was of no use to him beyond thinking that
he was swimming, but he also experienced a sense of relief, as if
he had finally discovered the key to the situation, and, as far as
he was concerned, it all came down to continuing his endless
journey, with an absence of organism in an absence of sea. The
illusion did not last. He was forced to roll from one side to the
other, like a boat adrift, in the water which gave him a body to
swim. What escape was there? To struggle in order not to be
carried away by the wave which was his arm? To go under?
To drown himself bitterly in himself? That would surely have
been the moment to stop, but a hope remained; he went on
swimming as if, deep within the restored core of his being, he
had discovered a new possibility. He swam, a monster without
fins. Under the giant microscope, he turned himself into an
enterprising mass of cilia and vibrations. The temptation took
on an entirely bizarre character when he sought to slip from the
drop of water into a region which was vague and yet infinitely

8

precise, a sort of holy place, so perfectly suited to him that it was enough for him to be there, to be; it was like an imaginary hollow which he entered because, before he was there, his imprint was there already. And so he made a last effort to fit completely inside. It was easy; he encountered no obstacles; he rejoined himself; he blended with himself, entering into this place which no one else could penetrate.

At last he had to come back. He found his way easily and his feet touched bottom at a place which some of the swimmers used for diving. The fatigue was gone. He still had a humming in his ears and a burning in his eyes, as might be expected after staying too long in the salt water. He became conscious of this as, turning toward the infinite sheet of water reflecting the sun, he tried to tell in which direction he had gone. At that point, there was a real mist before his sight, and he could pick out absolutely anything in this murky void which his gaze penetrated feverishly. Peering out, he discovered a man who was swimming far off, nearly lost below the horizon. At such a distance, the swimmer was always escaping him. He would see him, then lose sight of him, though he had the feeling that he was following his every move: not only perceiving him clearly all the time, but being brought near him in a completely intimate way, such that no other sort of contact could have brought him closer. He stayed a long time, watching and waiting. There was in this contemplation something painful which resembled the manifestation of an excessive freedom, a freedom obtained by breaking every bond. His face clouded over and took on an unusual expression.

HE NEVERTHELESS DECIDED to turn his back to the sea and entered a small woods where he lay down after taking a few steps. The day was about to end; scarcely any light remained, but it was still possible to see certain details of the landscape fairly clearly, in particular the hill which limited the horizon and which was glowing, unconcerned and free. What was disturbing to Thomas was the fact that he was lying there in the grass with the desire to remain there for a long time, although this position was forbidden to him. As night was falling he tried to get up, and, pushing against the ground with both hands, got one knee under him while the other leg dangled; then he made a sudden lurch and succeeded in placing himself entirely erect. So he was standing. As a matter of fact, there was an indecision in his way of being which cast doubt on what he was doing. And so, although his eyes were shut, it did not seem that he had given up seeing in the darkness, rather the contrary. Likewise, when he began to walk, one might have thought that it was not his legs, but rather his desire not to walk which pushed him forward. He went down into a sort of vault which at first he had believed to be rather large, but which very soon seemed to him extremely cramped: in front, in back, overhead, wherever he put out his hands, he collided brutally with a surface as hard as a stone wall; on all sides his way was barred, an insurmountable wall all around, and this wall was not the greatest obstacle for he had also to reckon on his will which was fiercely determined to let him sleep there in a passivity exactly like death. This was insane; in his uncertainty, feeling out the limits of the vaulted pit, he placed his body right up against the wall and waited. What dominated him was the sense of being pushed forward by his refusal to advance. So he was not very surprised, so clearly did

13

his anxiety allow him to see into the future, when, a little later, he saw himself carried a few steps further along. A few steps: it was unbelievable. His progress was undoubtedly more apparent than real, for this new spot was indistinguishable from the last, he encountered the same difficulties here, and it was in a sense the same place that he was moving away from out of terror of leaving it. At that moment, Thomas had the rashness to look around himself. The night was more somber and more painful than he could have expected. The darkness immersed everything; there was no hope of passing through its shadows, but one penetrated its reality in a relationship of overwhelming intimacy. His first observation was that he could still use his body, and particularly his eyes; it was not that he saw anything, but what he looked at eventually placed him in contact with a nocturnal mass which he vaguely perceived to be himself and in which he was bathed. Naturally, he formulated this remark only as a hypothesis, as a convenient point of view, but one to which he was obliged to have recourse only by the necessity of unraveling new circumstances. As he had no means of measuring time, he probably took some hours before accepting this way of looking at things, but, for him, it was as if fear had immediately conquered him, and it was with a sense of shame that he raised his head to accept the idea he had entertained: outside himself there was something identical to his own thought which his glance or his hand could touch. Repulsive fantasy. Soon the night seemed to him gloomier and more terrible than any night, as if it had in fact issued from a wound of thought which had ceased to think, of thought taken ironically as object by something other than thought. It was night itself. Images which constituted its darkness inundated him. He saw nothing, and, far from being distressed, he made this absence of vision the culmination of his sight. Useless for seeing, his eye took on extraordinary proportions, developed beyond measure, and, stretching out on the horizon, let the night penetrate its center in order to receive the day from it. And so, through this void, it was sight and the object of sight which mingled together. Not only did this eye which saw nothing apprehend something, it apprehended the cause of its vision. It saw as object that which prevented it from seeing. Its own glance entered into it as an image, just when this glance seemed the death of all image. New preoccupations came out of this for Thomas. His solitude no longer seemed so complete, and he even had the feeling that something real had knocked against him and was trying to slip inside. Perhaps he might have been able to interpret this feeling in some other way, but he always had to assume the worst. What excuses him is the fact that the impression was so clear and so painful that it was almost impossible not to give way to it. Even if he had questioned its truth, he would have had the greatest difficulty in not believing that something extreme and violent was happening, for from all evidence a foreign body had lodged itself in his pupil and was attempting to go further. It was strange, absolutely disturbing, all the more disturbing because it was not a small object, but whole trees, the whole woods still quivering and full of life. He felt this as a weakness which did him no credit. He no longer even paid attention to the details of events. Perhaps a man slipped in by the same opening, he could neither have affirmed nor denied it. It seemed to him that the waves were invading the sort of abyss which was himself. All this preoccupied him only slightly. He had no attention for anything but his hands, busy recognizing the beings mingled with himself, whose character they discerned by parts, a dog represented by an ear, a bird replacing the tree on which it sang. Thanks to these beings which indulged in acts which escaped all interpretation, edifices, whole cities were built, real cities made of emptiness and thousands of stones piled one on another, creatures rolling in blood and tearing arteries, playing the role of what Thomas had once called ideas and passions. And so fear took hold of him, and was in no way distinguishable from his corpse. Desire was this same corpse which opened its eyes and knowing itself to be dead climbed awkwardly back up into his mouth like an animal swallowed alive. Feelings occupied him, then devoured him. He was pressed in every part of his flesh by a thousand hands which were only his hand. A mortal anguish beat against his heart. Around his body, he knew that his thought, mingled with the night, kept watch. He knew with terrible certainty that it, too, was looking for a way to enter into him. Against his lips, in his mouth, it was forcing its way toward a monstrous union. Beneath his eyelids, it created a necessary sight. And at the same time it was furiously destroying the face it kissed. Prodigious cities, ruined fortresses disappeared. The stones were tossed outside. The trees were transplanted. Hands and corpses were taken away. Alone, the body of Thomas remained, deprived of its senses. And thought, having entered him again, exchanged contact with the void.

III

HE CAME BACK to the hotel for dinner. Of course, he could have taken his usual place at the main table, but he chose not to and kept to one side. Eating, at this point, was not without importance. On the one hand, it was tempting because he was demonstrating that he was still free to turn back; but on the other hand, it was bad because he risked recovering his freedom on too narrow a foundation. So he preferred to adopt a less frank attitude, and took a few steps forward to see how the others would accept his new manner. At first he listened; there was a confused, crude noise which one moment would become very loud and then lessen and become imperceptible. Yes, there was no mistake about it, it was the sound of conversation and, moreover, when the talking became quieter, he began to recognize some very simple words which seemed to be chosen so that he might understand them more easily. Still, unsatisfied by the words, he wanted to confront the people facing him, and made his way toward the table: once there, he remained silent, looking at these people who all seemed to him to have a certain importance. He was invited to sit down. He passed up the invitation. They encouraged him more strongly and an elderly woman turned to him asking if he had swum that afternoon. Thomas answered yes. There was a silence: a conversation was possible, then? Yet what he had said must not have been very satisfying, for the woman looked at him with a reproachful air and got up slowly, like someone who, not having been able to finish her task, has some sort of regret; however, this did not prevent her from giving the impression by her departure that she abandoned her role very willingly. Without thinking, Thomas took the free place, and once seated on a chair which seemed to him surprisingly low, but comfortable, he no longer dreamed of

19

anything but being served the meal which he had just refused. Wasn't it too late? He would have liked to consult those present on this point. Obviously, they were not showing themselves openly hostile toward him, he could even count on their good-will, without which he would have been incapable of remaining so much as a second in the room; but there was in their attitude also something underhanded which did not encourage confidence, nor even any sort of communication. As he observed his neighbor, Thomas was struck by her: a tall, blonde girl whose beauty awoke as he looked at her. She had seemed very pleased when he came to sit down beside her, but now she held herself with a sort of stiffness, with a childish wish to keep apart, all the stranger because he was moving closer to get some sign of encouragement from her. He nevertheless continued to stare at her, for, bathed in a superb light, her entire person drew him. Having heard someone call her *Anne* (in a very sharp tone), and seeing that she immediately raised her head, ready to answer, he decided to act and, with all his strength, struck the table. Tactical error, no doubt about it, unfortunate move: the result was immediate. Everyone, as if offended by a foolish action which could be tolerated only by ignoring it, closed themselves off in a reserve against which nothing could be done. Hours might pass now without rekindling the slightest hope, and the greatest proofs of docility were doomed to failure, as were all attempts at rebellion. And so it seemed the game was lost. It was then that, to precipitate matters, Thomas began to stare at each of them, even those who turned away, even those who, when their glance met his, looked at him now less than ever. No one would have been in a mood to put up for very long with this empty, demanding stare, asking for no one knew what, and wandering without control, but his neighbor took it particularly badly: she got up, arranged her hair, wiped her face and prepared to leave in silence. How tired her movements were! Just a moment ago, it was the light bathing her face, the highlights of her dress which made her presence so comforting, and now this brilliance was fading away. All that remained was a being whose fragility appeared in her faded beauty and who was even losing all reality, as if the contours of the body had been outlined not by the light, but by a diffuse phosphorescence emanating, one might believe, from the bones. No encouragement was to be hoped for any longer from her. Persevering indecently in this contemplation, one could only sink deeper and deeper into a feeling of loneliness where, however far one wished to go, one would only lose oneself and continue to lose oneself. Nevertheless, Thomas refused to let himself be convinced by simple impressions. He even turned back deliberately toward the girl (although he had really not taken his eyes off her). Around him, everyone was getting up from the table in a disagreeable disorder and confusion. He rose as well, and, in the room which was now plunged in deep shadow, measured with his eye the space he had to cross to get to the door. At this moment, everything lit up, the electric lights shone, illuminating the vestibule, shining outside where it seemed one must enter as if into a warm, soft thickness. At the same moment, the girl called him from outside in a determined tone, almost too loud, which had a domineering ring, though it was impossible to tell whether this impression came from the order given or only from the voice which took it too seriously. Thomas was very sensitive to this invitation and his first impulse was to obey, rushing into the empty space. Then, when the silence had absorbed the call, he

was no longer sure of having really heard his name and he contented himself with listening in the hope that he would be called
again. As he listened, he thought about the distance of all these
people, their absolute dumbness, their indifference. It was sheer
childishness to hope to see all these distances suppressed by a
single call. It was even humiliating and dangerous. At that point,
he raised his head and, having assured himself that everyone had
departed, he in turn left the room.

IV

THOMAS STAYED in his room to read. He was sitting with his hands joined over his brow, his thumbs pressing against his hairline, so deep in concentration that he did not make a move when anyone opened the door. Those who came in thought he was pretending to read, seeing that the book was always open to the same page. He was reading. He was reading with unsurpassable meticulousness and attention. In relation to every symbol, he was in the position of the male praying mantis about to be devoured by the female. They looked at each other. The words, coming forth from the book which was taking on the power of life and death, exercised a gentle and peaceful attraction over the glance which played over them. Each of them, like a half-closed eye, admitted the excessively keen glance which in other circumstances it would not have tolerated. And so Thomas slipped toward these corridors, approaching them defenselessly until the moment he was perceived by the very quick of the word. Even this was not fearful, but rather an almost pleasant moment he would have wished to prolong. The reader contemplated this little spark of life joyfully, not doubting that he had awakened it. It was with pleasure that he saw himself in this eye looking at him. The pleasure in fact became very great. It became so great, so pitiless that he bore it with a sort of terror, and in the intolerable moment when he had stood forward without receiving from his interlocutor any sign of complicity, he perceived all the strangeness there was in being observed by a word as if by a living being, and not simply by one word, but by all the words that were in that word, by all those that went with it and in turn contained other words, like a procession of angels opening out into the infinite to the very eye of the absolute. Rather than withdraw from a text whose defenses were so strong, he pitted all his strength in the will to seize it, obstinately refusing to withdraw his glance and still thinking himself a profound reader, even when the words were already taking hold of him and beginning to read him. He was seized, kneaded by intelligible hands, bitten by a vital tooth; he entered with his living body into the anonymous shapes of words, giving his substance to them, establishing their relationships, offering his being to the word "be". For hours he remained motionless, with, from time to time, the word "eyes" in place of his eyes: he was inert, captivated and unveiled. And even later when, having abandoned himself and, contemplating his book, he recognized himself with disgust in the form of the text he was reading, he retained the thought that (while, perched upon his shoulders, the word *He* and the word *I* were beginning their carnage) there remained within his person which was already deprived of its senses obscure words, disembodied souls and angels of words, which were exploring him deeply.

The first time he perceived this presence, it was night. By a light which came down through the shutters and divided the bed in two, he saw that the room was totally empty, so incapable of containing a single object that it was painful to the eye. The book was rotting on the table. There was no one walking in the room. His solitude was complete. And yet, sure as he was that there was no one in the room and even in the world, he was just as sure that someone was there, occupying his slumber, approaching him intimately, all around him and within him. On a naive impulse he sat up and sought to penetrate the night, trying with his hand to make light. But he was like a blind man who, hearing a noise, might run to light his lamp: nothing could make it possible for him to seize this presence in any shape or form. He was locked in combat with something inaccessible, foreign, something of which he could say: That doesn't exist . . . and which nevertheless filled him with terror as he sensed it wandering about in the region of his solitude. Having stayed up all night and all day with this being, as he tried to rest he was suddenly made aware that a second had replaced the first, just as inaccessible and just as obscure, and yet different. It was a modulation of that which did not exist, a different mode of being absent, another void in which he was coming to life. Now it was definitely true, someone was coming near him, standing not nowhere and everywhere, but a few feet away, invisible and certain. By an impulse which nothing might stop, and which nothing might quicken, a power with which he could not accept contact was coming to meet him. He wanted to flee. He threw himself into the corridor. Gasping and almost beside himself, he had taken only a few steps when he recognized the inevitable progress of the being coming toward him. He went back into the room. He barricaded the door. He waited, his back to the wall. But neither minutes nor hours put an end to his waiting. He felt ever closer to an ever more monstrous absence which took an infinite time to meet. He felt it closer to him every instant and kept ahead of it by an infinitely small but irreducible splinter of duration. He saw it, a horrifying being which was already pressing against him in space and, existing outside time, remained infinitely distant. Such unbearable waiting and anguish that they separated him from himself. A sort of Thomas left his body and went before the lurking threat. His eyes tried to look not in space but in duration, and in a point in time which did not yet exist. His hands sought to touch an impalpable and unreal body. It was such a painful effort that

27

this thing which was moving away from him and trying to draw him along as it went seemed the same to him as that which was approaching unspeakably. He fell to the ground. He felt he was covered with impurities. Each part of his body endured an agony. His head was forced to touch the evil, his lungs to breathe it in. There he was on the floor, writhing, reentering himself and then leaving again. He crawled sluggishly, hardly different from the serpent he would have wished to become in order to believe in the venom he felt in his mouth. He stuck his head under the bed, in a corner full of dust, resting among the reject-amenta as if in a refreshing place where he felt he belonged more properly than in himself. It was in this state that he felt himself bitten or struck, he could not tell which, by what seemed to him to be a word, but resembled rather a giant rat, an all-powerful beast with piercing eyes and pure teeth. Seeing it a few inches from his face, he could not escape the desire to devour it, to bring it into the deepest possible intimacy with himself. He threw himself on it and digging his fingernails into its entrails, sought to make it his own. The end of the night came. The light which shone through the shutters went out. But the struggle with the horrible beast, which had ultimately shown itself pos-sessed of incomparable dignity and splendor, continued for an immeasurable time. This struggle was terrible for the being ly-ing on the ground grinding his teeth, twisting his face, tearing out his eyes to force the beast inside; he would have seemed a madman, had he resembled a man at all. It was almost beautiful for this dark angel covered with red hair, whose eyes sparkled. One moment, the one thought he had triumphed and, with un-containable nausea, saw the word "innocence", which soiled him, slipping down inside him. The next moment, the other was devouring him in turn, dragging him out of the hole he had come from, then tossing him back, a hard, emptied body. Each time, Thomas was thrust back into the depths of his being by the very words which had haunted him and which he was pursuing as his nightmare and the explanation of his nightmare. He found that he was ever more empty, ever heavier; he no longer moved without infinite fatigue. His body, after so many struggles, became entirely opaque, and to those who looked at it, it gave the peaceful impression of sleep, though it had not ceased to be awake.

V

TOWARD THE MIDDLE of the second night, Thomas got up and went silently downstairs. No one noticed him with the exception of a nearly blind cat who, seeing the night change shape, ran after this new night which he did not see. After slipping into a tunnel where he did not recognize a single smell, this cat began to meow, forcing out from deep in his chest the raucous cry by which cats make it understood that they are sacred animals. He filled his lungs and howled. He drew from the idol he was becoming the incomprehensible voice which addressed itself to the night and spoke.

"What is happening?" said this voice. "The spirits with which I am usually in communication, the spirit that tugs at my tail when the bowl is full, the spirit that gets me up in the morning and puts me to bed in a soft comforter, and the most beautiful spirit of all, the one that meows and purrs and resembles me so closely that it is like my own spirit: they have all disappeared. Where am I now? If I feel gently with my paw, I find nothing. There's nothing anywhere. I'm at the very end of a gutter from which I can only fall. And that wouldn't scare me, falling. But the truth is that I can't even fall; no fall is possible; I am surrounded by a special void which repels me and which I wouldn't know how to cross over. Where am I then? Poor me. Once, by suddenly becoming a beast which might be cast into the fire with impunity, I used to penetrate secrets of the first order. By the flash of light which divided me, by the stroke of my claw, I knew lies and crimes before they were committed. And now I am a dull-eyed creature. I hear a monstrous voice by means of which I say what I say without knowing a single word of it all. I think, and my thoughts are as useless to me as hair standing on end or touching ears would be to the alien species I depend upon. Horror alone penetrates me. I turn round and round crying the cry of a terrible beast. I have a hideous affliction: my face feels as large as a spirit's face, with a smooth, insipid tongue, a blind man's tongue, a deformed nose incapable of prophecy, enormous eyes without that straight flame which permits us to see things in ourselves. My coat is splitting. That is doubtless the final operation. As soon as it is no longer possible even in this night, to draw a supernatural light from me by stroking my hair, it will be the end. I am already darker than the shadows. I am the night of night. Through the shadows from which I am distinguished because I am their shadow, I go to meet the over-cat. There is no fear in me now. My body, which is just like the body of a man, the body of the blessed, has kept its dimensions, but my head is enormous. There is a sound, a sound I have never heard before. A glow which seems to come from my body, though it is damp and lifeless, makes a circle around me which is like another body which I cannot leave. I begin to see a land-scape. As the darkness becomes more oppressive, a great pallid figure rises before me. I say 'me,' guided by a blind instinct, for ever since I lost the good, straight tail which was my rudder in this world, I am manifestly no longer myself. This head which will not stop growing, and rather than a head seems nothing but a glance, just what is it? I can't look at it without uneasiness. It's moving. It's coming closer. It is turned directly toward me and, pure glance though it is, it gives me the terrible impression that it doesn't see me. This feeling is unbearable. If I still had any hair, I would feel it standing up all over my body. But in my condition I no longer have even the means to experience the fear I feel. I am dead, dead. This head, my head, no longer even sees me, because I am annihilated. For it is I looking at myself and

34

not perceiving myself. Oh over-cat whom I have become for an instant to establish the fact of my decease, I shall now disappear for good. First of all, I cease being a man. I again become a cold, uninhabitable little cat stretched out on the earth. I howl one more time. I take a last look at this vale which is about to be closed up, and where I see a man, himself an over-cat as well. I hear him scratching the ground, probably with his claws. What is called the beyond is finished for me."

On his knees, his back bent, Thomas was digging in the earth. Around him extended several ditches on the edges of which the day was packed down. For the seventh time, leaving the mark of his hands in the soil, he was slowly preparing a great hole, which he was enlarging to his size. And while he was digging it, the hole, as if it had been filled by dozens of hands, then by arms and finally by the whole body, offered a resistance to his work which soon became insurmountable. The tomb was full of a being whose absence it absorbed. An immovable corpse was lodged there, finding in this absence of shape the perfect shape of its presence. It was a drama the horror of which was felt by the village folk in their sleep. As soon as the grave was finished, when Thomas threw himself into it with a huge stone tied around his neck, he crashed into a body a thousand times harder than the soil, the very body of the gravedigger who had already entered the grave to dig it. This grave which was exactly his size, his shape, his thickness, was like his own corpse, and every time he tried to bury himself in it, he was like a ridiculous dead person trying to bury his body in his body. There was, then, henceforth, in all the sepulchers where he might have been able to take his place, in all the feelings which are also tombs for the dead, in this annihilation through which he was dying without permitting himself to be thought dead, there was another dead person who was there first, and who, identical with himself, drove the ambiguity of Thomas's life and death to the extreme limit. In this subterranean night into which he had descended with cats and the dreams of cats, a double wrapped in bands, its senses sealed with the seven seals, its spirit absent, occupied his place, and this double was the unique one with which no compromise was possible, since it was the same as himself, realized in the absolute void. He leaned over this glacial tomb. Just as the man who is hanging himself, after kicking away the stool on which he stood, the final shore, rather than feeling the leap which he is making into the void feels only the rope which holds him, held to the end, held more than ever, bound as he had never been before to the existence he would like to leave, even so Thomas felt himself, at the moment he knew himself to be dead, absent, completely absent from his death. Neither his body, which left in the depths of himself that coldness which comes from contact with a corpse and which is not coldness but absence of contact, nor the darkness, which seeped from all his pores and even when he was visible made it impossible to use any sense, intuition or thought to see him, nor the fact that by no right could he pass for living, sufficed to make him pass for dead. And it was not a misunderstanding. He was really dead and at the same time rejected from the reality of death. In death itself, he was deprived of death, a horribly destroyed man, stopped in the midst of nothingness by his own image, by this Thomas running before him, bearer of extinguished torches, who was like the existence of the very last death. Already, as he still leaned over this void where he saw his image in the total absence of images, seized by the most violent vertigo possible, a

36

vertigo which did not make him fall but prevented him from falling and rendered impossible the fall it rendered inevitable, already the earth was shrinking around him and night, a night which no longer responded to anything, which he did not see and whose reality he sensed only because it was less real than himself, surrounded him. In every way, he was invaded by the feeling of being at the heart of things. Even on the surface of this earth which he could not penetrate, he was within this earth, whose insides touched him on all sides. On all sides, night closed him in. He saw, he heard the core of an infinity where he was bound by the very absence of limits. He felt as an oppressive existence the nonexistence of this valley of death. Little by little the emanations of an acrid and damp leaf-mold reached him. Like a man waking up alive in his coffin, terrified, he saw the impalpable earth where he floated transformed into an air without air, filled with smells of the earth, of rotten wood, of damp cloth. Now truly buried, he discovered himself, beneath accumulated layers of a material resembling plaster, in a hole where he was smothering. He was soaked in an icy medium among objects which were crushing him. If he still existed, it was to recognize the impossibility of living again, here in this room full of funereal flowers and spectral light. Suffocating, he managed to breathe again. He again discovered the possibility of walking, of seeing, of crying out, deep within a prison where he was confined in impenetrable silence and darkness. What a strange horror was his, as, passing the last barriers, he appeared at the narrow gate of his sepulcher, not risen but dead, and with the certainty of being snatched at once from death and from life. He walked, a painted mummy; he looked at the sun which was making an effort to put a smiling, lively expression on its

37

indifferent face. He walked, the only true Lazarus, whose very death was resurrected. He went forward, passing beyond the last shadows of night without losing any of his glory, covered with grass and earth, walking at an even pace beneath the falling stars, the same pace which, for those men who are not wrapped in a winding-sheet, marks the ascent toward the most precious point in life.

VI

ANNE SAW HIM coming without surprise, this inevitable being in whom she recognized the one she might try in vain to escape, but would meet again every day. Each time, he came straight to her, following with an inflexible pace a path laid straight over the sea, the forests, even the sky. Each time, when the world was emptied of everything but the sun and this motionless being standing at her side, Anne, enveloped in his silent immobility, carried away by this profound insensitivity which revealed her, feeling all the calm of the universe condensing in her through him, just as the sparkling chaos of the ultimate noon was resounding, mingled with the silence, pressed by the greatest peace, not daring to make a move or to have a thought, seeing herself burned, dying, her eyes, her cheeks aflame, mouth half-open exhaling, as a last breath, her obscure forms into the glare of the sun, perfectly transparent in death beside this opaque corpse which stood by, becoming ever more dense, and, more silent than silence, undermined the hours and deranged time. A just and sovereign death, inhuman and shameful moment which began anew each day, and from which she could not escape. Each day he returned at the same time to the same place. And it was precisely the same moment, the same garden as well. With the ingenuousness of Joshua stopping the sun to gain time, Anne believed that things were going on. But the terrible trees, dead in their green foliage which could not dry out, the birds which flew above her without, alas, deceiving anyone or succeeding in making themselves pass for living, stood solemn guard over the horizon and made her begin again eternally the scene she had lived the day before. Nevertheless, that day (as if a corpse borne from one bed to another were really changing place) she arose, walked before Thomas and drew him toward the little woods

41

nearby, along a road on which those who came from the other direction saw him recede, or thought he was motionless. In fact, he was really walking and, with a body like the others, though three-quarters consumed, he penetrated a region where, if he himself disappeared, he immediately saw the others fall into another nothingness which placed them further from him than if they had continued to live. On this road, each man he met died. Each man, if Thomas turned away his eyes, died with him a death which was not announced by a single cry. He looked at them, and already he saw them lose all resemblance beneath his glance, with a tiny wound in the forehead through which their face escaped. They did not disappear, but they did not appear again. As far away as they became visible, they were shapeless and mute. Nearer, if he touched them, if he directed toward them not his glance, but the glance of this dazzling and invisible eye which he was, every moment, completely . . . and nearer yet, almost blending with them, taking them either for his shadow or for dead souls, breathing them, licking them, coating himself with their bodies, he received not the slightest sensation, not the slightest image, as empty of them as they were empty of him. Finally they passed by. They went away, definitively. They slipped down a vertiginous slope toward a country whence nothing was any longer visible, except perhaps, like a great trail of light, their last phosphorescent stare on the horizon. It was a terrible and mysterious blast. Behind him there were no more words, no silence, no backward and no forward. The space surrounding him was the opposite of space, infinite thought in which those who entered, their heads veiled, existed only for nothing.

In this abyss Anne alone resisted. Dead, dissolved in the

closest thing to the void, she yet found there the debris of beings with whom she maintained, in the midst of the holocaust, a sort of familial resemblance in her features. If he came straight up to her, brutally, to surprise her, she always presented him a face. She changed without ceasing to be Anne. She was Anne, having no longer the slightest resemblance to Anne. In her face and in all her features, while she was completely identical to another, she remained the same, Anne, Anne complete and undeniable. On his path, he saw her coming like a spider which was identical to the girl and, among the vanished corpses, the emptied men, walked through the deserted world with a strange peace, last descendant of a fabulous race. She walked with eight enormous legs as if on two delicate ones. Her black body, her ferocious look which made one think she was about to bite when she was about to flee, were not different from the clothed body of Anne, from the delicate air she had when one tried to see her close up. She came forward jerkily, now devouring space in a few bounds, now lying down on the path, brooding it, drawing it from herself like an invisible thread. Without even drawing in her limbs, she entered the space surrounding Thomas. She approached irresistibly. She stopped before him. Then, that day, seized by this incredible bravery and perseverance, recognizing in her something carefree which could not disappear in the midst of trials and which resounded like a memory of freedom, seeing her get up on her long legs, hold herself at the level of his face to communicate with him, secreting a whirlwind of nuances, of odors and thoughts, he turned and looked bitterly behind him, like a traveler who, having taken a wrong turn, moves away, then draws within himself and finally disappears in the thought of his journey. Yes, this woods, he recognized it.

43

And this declining sun, he recognized that, and these trees drying out and these green leaves turning black. He tried to shake the enormous weight of his body, a missing body whose illusion he bore like a borrowed body. He needed to feel the factitious warmth which radiated from himself as from an alien sun, to hear the breath flowing from a false source, to listen to the beating of a false heart. And her, did he recognize her, this dead person on guard behind a hideous resemblance, ready to appear as she was, in the atmosphere studded with little mirrors where every one of her features survived? "It's you?" he asked. Immediately he saw a flame in a pair of eyes, a sad, cold flame on a face. He shuddered in this unknown body while Anne, feeling a sad spirit entering into her, a funereal youthfulness she was sworn to love, believed she was again becoming herself.

VII

ANNE HAD A FEW DAYS of great happiness. And she had never even dreamed of a simpler happiness, a lovelier tenderness. For her, he was suddenly a being she possessed without danger. If she took hold of him, it was with the greatest freedom. As for his head, he abandoned it to her. His words, before they were spoken, might as well have been in one mouth as the other, so completely did he let her do as she wished. In this way in which Anne played with his entire person and in the absence of risk which permitted her to treat this strange body as if it belonged to her, there was a frivolousness so perilous that anyone would have been pained at it. But she saw in him only a futile mouth, empty glances, and, rather than feeling uneasy at the realization that a man she could not approach, whom she could not dream of making speak, consented to roll his head in her lap, she enjoyed it. It was, on her part, a way to act which was difficult to justify. From one moment to the next one might anticipate, between these bodies bound so intimately together by such fragile bonds, a contact which would reveal in a terrible way their lack of bonds. The more he withdrew within himself, the more she came frivolously forward. He attracted her, and she buried herself in the face whose contours she still thought she was caressing. Did she act so imprudently because she thought she was dealing with someone inaccessible, or, on the other hand, with someone too easy to approach? Her stare was fixed on him . . . was this an impudent game, or a desperate one? Her words became moist, even her weakest movements glued her against him, while within her swelled up the pocket of humors from which she would perhaps, at the proper moment, draw an extreme power of adhesion. She covered herself with suction-cups. Within and without, she was no more than wounds try-

47

ing to heal, flesh being grafted. And, despite such a change, she continued to play and to laugh. As she held out her hand to him she said: "Really, who could you be?"

Properly speaking, there was no question in this remark. Distracted as she was, how could she have interrogated a being whose existence was a terrible question posed to herself? But she seemed to find it surprising and slightly shocking, yes, really shocking, not yet to be able, not to understand him (which in itself would have been extremely presumptuous), but (and this time the rashness went beyond all limits) to get information about him. And this boldness was not enough for her, for the regret she felt at not knowing him, rather than trying to justify itself in its bizarre form through the violence and madness of its expression, emerged rather as a relaxed and almost indifferent regret. It was, beneath the benign appearance all such operations have, an actual attempt to tempt God. She looked him right in the face: "But, what are you?"

Although she did not expect to hear him answer and even if she were sure that he would not answer she would not in fact have questioned him, there was such a presumption in her manner of assuming that he could give an answer (of course, he would not answer, she did not ask him to answer, but, by the question she had posed him personally and relating to his person, she acted as if she might interpret his silence as an accidental refusal to answer, as an attitude which might change one day or another), it was such a crude way to treat the impossible that Anne had suddenly revealed to her the terrible scene she was throwing herself into blindfolded, and in an instant, waking from her sleep, she perceived all the consequences of her act and the madness of her conduct. Her first thought was to pre-

48

vent him from answering. For the great danger, now that by an inconsiderate and arbitrary act she had just treated him as a being one might question, was that he might in turn act like a being that might answer and make his answer understood. She felt this threat deposited in the depths of her self, in the place of the words she had spoken. He was already grasping the hand held out to him. He seized it cruelly, giving Anne to believe that he understood her reasons, and that after all there was in fact a possibility of contact between them. Now that she was sure that, pitilessly unrelenting as he was, if he spoke he would say everything there was to say without hiding anything from her, telling her everything so that when he stopped speaking his silence, the silence of a being that has nothing more to give and yet has given nothing, would be even more terrifying, now she was sure that he would speak. And this certainty was so great that he appeared to her as if he had already spoken. He surrounded her, like an abyss. He revolved about her. He entranced her. He was going to devour her by changing the most unexpected words into words she would no longer be able to expect.

"What I am. . . ."

"Be quiet."

It was late, and knowing that hours and days no longer concerned anyone but her, she cried louder in the shadows. She came near and lay down before the window. Her face melted, and again closed itself. When the darkness was complete, leaning in her tattered way toward the one she now called, in her new language drawn from the depths, her friend, without worrying about her own state she wanted (like a drunkard with no legs explaining to himself by his drunkenness the fact that he can no longer walk), she wanted to see why her relations with this dead man no longer seemed to be advancing. As low as she had fallen, and probably because from that level she perceived that there was a difference between them and a huge difference, but not such that their relationship must always be doomed, she was suddenly suspicious of all the politenesses they had exchanged. In the folds where she hid herself, she told herself with a profoundly sophisticated air that she would not allow herself to be deceived by the appearance of this perfectly lovable young man, and it was with deep pain that she recalled his welcoming manner and the ease with which she approached him. If she did not go so far as to suspect him of hypocrisy (she might complain, she might cry miserably because he kept her twenty fathoms below the truth in brilliant and empty words; but it never came into her head, in spite of her sullen efforts to speak of herself and of him in the same words, that there might be, in what she called the character of Thomas, any duplicity), it was because, just by turning her head, in the silence in which he necessarily existed, she perceived him to be so impenetrable that she saw clearly how ridiculous it would have been to call him insincere. He did not deceive her, and yet she was deceived by him. Treachery revolved about them, so much the more terrible because it was *she* who was betraying *him*, and she was deceiving herself at the same time with no hope of putting an end to this aberration since, not knowing who he was, she always found someone else beside her. Even the night increased her error, even time which made her try again and again without reprieve the same things, which she undertook with a fierce and humiliated air. It was a story emptied of events, emptied to the point that every memory and all perspective were eliminated, and nevertheless drawing from this absence its inflexible direction which seemed to carry everything away in the irresistible movement toward an imminent catastrophe. What was going to happen? She did not know, but devoting her entire life to waiting, her impatience melted into the hope of participating in a general cataclysm in which, at the same time as the beings themselves, the distances which separate beings would be destroyed.

VIII

IT WAS IN THIS NEW STATE that, feeling herself becoming an enormous, immeasurable reality on which she fed her hopes, like a monster revealed to no one, not even to herself, she became still bolder and, keeping company with Thomas, came to attribute to more and more penetrable motives the difficulties of her relationship with him, thinking, for example, that what was abnormal was that nothing could be discovered about his life and that in every circumstance he remained anonymous and without a history. Once she had started in this direction, there was no chance of her stopping herself in time. It would have been just as well to say whatever came into one's head with no other intention than to put the words to the test. But, far from condescending to observe these precautions, she saw fit, in a language whose solemnity contrasted with her miserable condition, to rise to a height of profanation which hung on the apparent truth of her words. What she said to him took the form of direct speech. It was a cry full of pride which resounded in the sleepless night with the very character of dream.

"Yes," she said, "I would like to see you when you are alone. If ever I could be before you and completely absent from you, I would have a chance to meet you. Or rather I know that I would not meet you. The only possibility I would have to diminish the distance between us would be to remove myself to an infinite distance. But I am infinitely far away now, and can go no further. As soon as I touch you, Thomas. . . ."

Hardly out of her mouth, these words carried her away: she saw him, he was radiant. Her head thrown back, a soft noise rose from her throat which drove all memories away; there was no need, now, to cry out . . . her eyes closed, her spirit was intoxicated; her breathing became slow and deep, her hands came together: this should reasonably have continued forever. But, as if the silence were also an invitation to return (for it bound her to nothing), she let herself go, opened her eyes, recognized the room and, once again, everything had to be begun anew. This deception, the fact that she did not have the desired explanation, left her unmoved. She certainly could no longer think that he would reveal to her what was, to her, a sort of secret, and for him had in no way the quality of a secret. On the contrary, clinging to the idea that what she might say would endure, in spite of everything, she was determined to communicate to him the fact that, though she was not unaware of the extraordinary distance which separated them, she would obstinately maintain contact with him to the very end, for, if there was something shameless in her concern to say that what she was doing was insane, and that nevertheless she was doing it fully conscious of the situation, there was something very tempting in it as well. But could one even believe that, infantile as that might be, she could do it on her own? Speak, yes, she could start to speak, with the sense of guilt of an accomplice betraying his companion, not in admitting what he knows—he knows nothing— but in admitting what he does not know, for she did not have it within her means to say anything true or even apparently true; and nevertheless what she said, without allowing her to perceive the truth in any sense, without the compensation of throwing the slightest light on the enigma, chained her as heavily, perhaps more heavily, than if she had revealed the very heart of secrets. Far from being able to slip into the lost pathways where she would have had the hope of coming near to him, she only went astray in her travels and led forth an illusion which, even in her eyes, was only an illusion. Despite the dimming of her perspective she suspected that her project was puerile and that further-more she was committing a great mistake with nothing to gain from it, although she also had this thought (and in fact this was just the mistake): that the moment she made a mistake because of him or relating to him, she created between them a link he would have to reckon with. But she nevertheless guessed how dangerous it was to see in him a being who had experienced events no doubt different from others, but fundamentally anal-ogous to all the others, to plunge him into the same water which flowed over her. It was not, at any event, a small imprudence to mix time, her personal time, with that which detested time, and she knew that no good for her own childhood could emerge from the caricature—and if the image had been a perfect one it would have been worse—of childhood which would be given by one who could have no historical character. So the uneasiness rose in her, as if time had already been corrupted, as if all her past, again placed in question, had been offered up in a barren and inevitably guilty future. And she could not even console herself in the thought that, since everything she had to say was arbitrary, the risk itself was illusory. On the contrary she knew, she felt, with an anguish which seemed to threaten her very life but which was more precious than her life, that, though she might say nothing true no matter how she might speak, she was exposing herself (in retaining only one version among so many others) to the danger of rejecting seeds of truth which would be sacrificed. And she felt further, with an anxiety which threat-ened her purity but which brought her a new purity, that she was going to be forced (even if she tried to cut herself off behind the most arbitrary and most innocent evocation) to introduce something serious into her tale, an impenetrable and terrible

57

reminiscence, so that, as this false figure emerged from the shadows, acquiring through a useless meticulousness a greater and greater precision and a more and more artificial one, she herself, the narrator, already condemned and delivered into the hands of the devils, would bind herself unpardonably to the true figure, of which she would know nothing.

"What you are . . . ," she said. . . . And as she spoke these words, she semed to dance around him and, fleeing him at the same time, to push him into an imaginary wolf-trap. "What you are. . . ."

She could not speak, and yet she was speaking. Her tongue vibrated in such a way that she seemed to express the meanings of words without the words themselves. Then, suddenly, she let herself be carried away by a rush of words which she pronounced almost beneath her breath, with varied inflections, as if she wanted only to amuse herself with sounds and bursts of syllables. She gave the impression that, speaking a language whose infantile character prevented it from being taken for a language, she was making the meaningless words seem like incomprehensible ones. She said nothing, but to say nothing was for her an all too meaningful mode of expression, beneath which she succeeded in saying still less. She withdrew indefinitely from her babbling to enter into yet another, less serious babbling, which she nevertheless rejected as too serious, preparing herself by an endless retreat beyond all seriousness for repose in absolute puerility, until her vocabulary, through its nullity, took on the appearance of a sleep which was the very voice of seriousness. Then, as if in the depths she had suddenly felt herself under the surveillance of an implacable consciousness, she leaped back, cried out, opened terribly clairvoyant eyes and, halting her tale an instant: "No," she said, "it's not that. What you really are . . ."

She herself took on a puerile and frivolous appearance. From beneath the murky look which had veiled her face for a few moments came forth expressions which made her seem distracted. She presented such a delicate appearance that, looking at her, it was impossible to fix one's attention on her features, or on the whole of her person. It was that much more difficult to remember what she said and to attach any meaning to it. It was impossible even to know about whom she was talking. One moment she seemed to be talking to Thomas, but the very fact that she was talking to him made it impossible to perceive her actual interlocutor. The next moment she was talking to no one, and, vain as her lisping was at that point, there came a moment when, brought forward by this endless wandering before a reality without reason, she stopped suddenly, emerging from the depths of her frivolity with a hideous expression. The issue was still the same. It was vain for her to search out her route at the ends of the earth and lose herself in infinite digressions—and the voyage might last her entire life; she knew that she was coming closer every minute to the instant when it would be necessary not only to stop but to abolish her path, either having found what she should not have found, or eternally unable to find it. And it was impossible for her to give up her project. For how could she be silent, she whose language was several degrees below silence? By ceasing to be there, ceasing to live? These were just more ridiculous strategies, for through her death, closing off all the exits, she would only have precipitated the eternal race in the labyrinth, from which she retained the hope of escape as long as she had the perspective of time. And she no longer saw that she was coming imperceptibly closer to Thomas. She followed him, step by step, without realizing it, or if she realized it, then, wanting to leave him, to flee him, she had to make a greater effort. Her exhaustion became so overwhelming that she contented herself with mimicking her flight and stayed glued to him, her eyes flowing with tears, begging, imploring him to put an end to this situation, still trying, leaning over this mouth, to formulate words to continue her narrative at any cost, the same narrative she would have wished to devote her last measure of strength to interrupting and stifling.

It was in this state of abandonment that she allowed herself to be carried along by the feeling of duration. Gently, her fingers drew together, her steps left her and she slipped into a pure water where, from one instant to the next, crossing eternal currents, she seemed to pass from life to death, and worse, from death to life, in a tormented dream which was already absorbed in a peaceful dream. Then suddenly with the noise of a tempest she entered into a solitude made of the suppression of all space, and, torn violently by the call of the hours, she unveiled herself. It was as if she were in a green valley where, invited to be the personal rhythm, the impersonal cadence of all things, she was becoming with her age and her youth, the age, the old age, of others. First she climbed down into the depths of a day totally foreign to human days, and, full of seriousness, entering into the intimacy of pure things, then rising up toward sovereign time, drowned among the stars and the spheres, far from knowing the peace of the skies she began to tremble and to experience pain. It was during this night and this eternity that she prepared herself to become the time of men. Endlessly, she wandered along the empty corridors lit by the reflected light of a source which always hid itself and which she pursued without love, with the obstinacy of an already lost soul incapable of seizing again the sense of these metamorphoses and the goal of this silent walk. But, when she passed before a door which looked like Thomas's, recognizing that the tragic debate was still going on, she knew then that she was no longer arguing with him with words and thoughts, but with the very time she was espousing. Now, each second, each sigh—and it was herself, nothing other than herself—dumbly attacked the unconcerned life he held up to her. And in each of his reasonings, more mysterious still than his existence, he experienced the mortal presence of the adversary, of this time without which, eternally immobilized, unable to come from the depths of the future, he would have been condemned to see the light of life die out on his desolate peak, like the prophetic eagle of dreams. So he reasoned with the absolute contradictor at the heart of his argument, he thought with the enemy and the subject of all thought in the depths of his thought, his perfect antagonist, this *time*, Anne, and mysteriously receiving her within himself he found himself for the first time at grips with a serious conversation. It was in this situation that she penetrated as a vague shape into the existence of Thomas. Everything there appeared desolate and mournful. Deserted shores where deeper and deeper absences, abandoned by the eternally departed sea after a magnificent shipwreck, gradually decomposed. She passed through strange dead cities where, rather than petrified shapes, mummified circumstances, she found a necropolis of movements, silences, voids; she hurled herself against the extraordinary sonority of nothingness which is made of the reverse of sound, and before her spread forth wondrous falls, dreamless sleep, the fading away which buries the dead in a life of dream, the death by which every man, even the weakest spirit, becomes

61

spirit itself. In this exploration which she had undertaken so naively, believing that she might find the last word on herself, she recognized herself passionately in search of the absence of Anne, of the most absolute nothingness of Anne. She thought she understood—oh cruel illusion—that the indifference which flowed the length of Thomas like a lonely stream came from the infiltration, in regions she should never have penetrated, of the fatal absence which had succeeded in breaking all the dams, so that, wanting now to discover this naked absence, this pure negative, the equivalent of pure light and deep desire, she had, in order to reach it, to yoke herself to severe trials. For lives on end she had to polish her thought, to relieve it of all that which made of it a miserable bric-a-brac, the mirror which admires itself, the prism with its interior sun: she needed an I without its glassy solitude, without this eye so long stricken with strabism, this eye whose supreme beauty is to be as crosseyed as possible, the eye of the eye, the thought of thought. One might have thought of her as running into the sun and at every turn of the path tossing into an ever more voracious abyss an eternally poorer and more rarified Anne. One would have confused her with this very abyss where, remaining awake in the midst of sleep, her spirit free of knowing, without light, bringing nothing to think in her meeting with thought, she prepared to go out so far in front of herself that on contact with the absolute nakedness, miraculously passing beyond, she could recognize therein her pure, her very own transparency. Gently, armed only with the name Anne which must serve her to return to the surface after the dive, she let the tide of the first and crudest absences rise—absence of sound silence, absence of being death—but after this so tepid and facile nothingness which Pascal, though already terrified, inhabited, she was seized by the diamond absences, the absence of silence, the absence of death, where she could no longer find any foothold except in ineffable notions, indefinable somethings, sphinxes of unheard rumblings, vibrations which burst the ether of the most shattering sounds, and, exceeding their energy, explode the sounds themselves. And she fell among the major circles, analogous to those of Hell, passing, a ray of pure reason, by the critical moment when for a very short instant one must remain in the absurd and, having left behind that which can still be represented, indefinitely add absence to absence and to the absence of absence and to the absence of the absence of absence and, thus, with this vacuum machine, desperately create the void. At this instant the real fall begins, the one which abolishes itself, nothingness incessantly devoured by a purer nothingness. But at this limit Anne became conscious of the madness of her undertaking. Everything she had thought she had suppressed of herself, she was certain she was finding it again, entire. At this moment of supreme absorption, she recognized at the deepest point of her thought a thought, the miserable thought that she was Anne, the living, the blonde, and, oh horror, the intelligent. Images petrified her, gave birth to her, produced her. A body was bestowed on her, a body a thousand times more beautiful than her own, a thousand times more body; she was visible, she radiated from the most unchangeable matter: at the center of nullified thought she was the superior rock, the crumbly earth, without nitrogen, that from which it would not even have been possible to create Adam; she was finally going to avenge herself by hurling herself against the incommunicable with this grossest, ugliest body, this body of mud, with this vulgar idea that she wanted to vomit, that she was vomiting, bearing to the marvelous absence her portion of excrement. It was at that moment that at the heart of the unheard a shattering noise rang out and she began to howl "Anne, Anne" in a furious voice. At the heart of indifference, she burst into flame, a complete torch with all her passion, her hate for Thomas, her love for Thomas. At the heart of nothingness, she intruded as a triumphal presence and hurled herself there, a corpse, an inassimilable nothingness, Anne, who still existed and existed no longer, a supreme mockery to the thought of Thomas.

IX

WHEN SHE CAME AROUND, entirely speechless now, refusing any expression to her eyes as well as her lips, still stretched out on the ground, the silence showed her so united with silence that she embraced it furiously like another nature, whose intimacy would have overwhelmed her with disgust. It seemed as if, during this night, she had assimilated something imaginary which was a burning thorn to her and forced her to shove her own existence outside like some foul excrement. Motionless against the wall, her body had mingled with the pure void, thighs and belly united to a nothingness with neither sex nor sexual parts, hands convulsively squeezing an absence of hands, face drinking in what was neither breath nor mouth, she had transformed herself into another body whose life—supreme penury and indigence—had slowly made her become the totality of that which she could not become. There where her body was, her sleeping head, there too was body without head, head without body, body of wretchedness. Doubtless nothing had changed about her appearance, but the glance one might direct toward her which showed her to be like anyone else was utterly unimportant, and, precisely because it was impossible to identify her, it was in the perfect resemblance of her features, in the glaze of naturalness and sincerity laid down by the night, that the horror of seeing her just as she had always been, without the least change, while it was certain that she was completely changed, found its source. Forbidden spectacle. While one might have been able to bear the sight of a monster, there was no cold-bloodedness that could hold out against the impression created by this face on which, for hours, in an investigation which came to nothing, the eye sought to distinguish a sign of strangeness or bizarreness. What one saw, with its familiar naturalness, be-

67

came, by the simple fact that manifestly it was not what one should have seen, an enigma which finally not only blinded the eye but made it experience toward this image an actual nausea, an expulsion of detritus of all sorts which the glance forced upon itself in trying to seize in this object something other than what it could see there. In fact, if what was entirely changed in an identical body—the sense of disgust imposed on all the senses forced to consider themselves insensitive—if the ungraspable character of the new person that had devoured the old and left her as she was, if this mystery buried in absence of mystery had not explained the silence which flowed from the sleeping girl, one would have been tempted to search out in such calm some indication of the tragedy of illusions and lies in which the body of Anne had wrapped itself. There was in fact something terribly suspicious about her mutism. That she should not speak, that in her motionlessness she should retain the discretion of someone who remains silent even in the intimacy of her dreams, all this was, finally, natural, and she was not about to betray herself, to expose herself, through this sleep piled upon sleep. But her silence did not even have the right to silence, and through this absolute state were expressed at once the complete unreality of Anne and the unquestionable and indemonstrable presence of this unreal Anne, from whom there emanated, by this silence, a sort of terrible humor which one became uneasily conscious of. As if there had been a crowd of intrigued and moved spectators, she turned to ridicule the possibility that one might see her, and a sense of ridicule came also from this wall against which she had stretched herself out in a way one might have taken (what stupidity) for sleep, and from this room where she was, wrapped in a linen coat, and where the day was begin-

68

ning to penetrate with the laughable intention of putting an end to the night by giving the password: "Life goes on." Even alone, there was around her a sad and insatiable curiosity, a dumb interrogation which, taking her as object, bore also, vaguely, on everything, so that she existed as a problem capable of producing death, not, like the sphinx, by the difficulty of the enigma, but by the temptation which she offered of resolving the problem in death.

When day had come, as she was waking up, one might have thought she had been drawn from sleep by the day. However, the end of the night did not explain the fact that she had opened her eyes, and her awakening was only a slow exhausting, the final movement toward rest: what made it impossible for her to sleep was the action of a force which, far from being opposed to the night, might just as well have been called nocturnal. She saw that she was alone, but though she could rise only in the world of solitude, this isolation remained foreign to her, and, in the passive state where she remained, it was not important that her solitude should burst in her like something she did not need to feel and which drew her into the eternally removed domain of day. Not even the sadness was any longer felt as present. It wandered about her in a blind form. It came forward within the sphere of resignation, where it was impossible for it to strike or hit. Crossing over betrayed fatality, it came right to the heart of the young woman and touched her with the feeling of letting go, with absence of consciousness into which she leapt with the greatest abandon. From this moment on, not a single desire came to her to elucidate her situation in any way, and love was reduced to the impossibility of expressing and experiencing that love. Thomas came in. But the presence of Thomas no longer had any importance in itself. On the contrary, it was terrible to see to what extent the desire to enjoy this presence, even in the most ordinary way, had faded. Not only was every motive for clear communication destroyed, but to Anne it seemed that the mystery of this being had passed into her own heart, the very place where it could no longer be seized except as an eternally badly formulated question. And he, on the contrary, in the silent indifference of his coming, gave an impression of offensive clarity, without the feeblest, the most reassuring sign of a secret. It was in vain that she looked at him with the troubled looks of her fallen passion. It was as the least obscure man in the world that he came forth from the night, bathed in transparency by the privilege of being above any interrogation, a transfigured but trivial character from whom the problems were now separating themselves, just as she also saw herself turned away from him by this dramatically empty spectacle, turned away upon herself where there was neither richness nor fullness but the oppressiveness of a dreary satiety, the certainty that there should evolve no other drama than the playing out of a day where despair and hope would be drowned, the useless waiting having become, through the suppression of all ends and of time itself, a machine whose mechanism had for its sole function the measurement, by a silent exploration, of the empty movement of its various parts. She went down into the garden and, there, seemed to disengage herself at least in part from the condition into which the events of the night had thrown her. The sight of the trees stunned her. Her eyes clouded over. What was striking now was the extreme weakness she showed. There was no resistance left in her organism, and with her transparent skin, the great pallor of her glances, she semed to tremble with exhaustion whenever

70

anyone or anything approached her. In fact one might have wondered how she could stand the contact of the air and the cries of the birds. By the way she oriented herself in the garden, one was almost sure that she was in another garden: not that she walked like a somnambulist in the midst of the images of her slumber, but she managed to proceed across the field full of life, resounding and sunlit, to a worn-out field, mournful and extinguished, which was a second version of the reality she traveled through. Just when one saw her stop, out of breath and breathing with difficulty the excessively fresh, cool air which blew against her, she was penetrating a rarified atmosphere in which, to get back her breath, it was enough to stop breathing entirely. While she was walking with difficulty along the path where she had to lift up her body with each step, she was entering, a body without knees, onto a path in every way like the first, but where she alone could go. This landscape relaxed her, and she felt the same consolation there as if, overturning from top to bottom the illusory body whose intimacy oppressed her, she might have been able to exhibit to the sun which threw light on her like a faint star, in the form of her visible chest, her folded legs, her dangling arms, the bitter disgust which was piecing together an absolutely hidden second person deep within her. In this ravaged day, she could confess the revulsion and fright whose vastness could be circumscribed by no image, and she succeeded almost joyously in forcing from her belly the inexpressible feelings (fantastic creatures having in turn the shape of her face, of her skeleton, of her entire body) which had drawn within her the entire world of repulsive and unbearable things, through the horror that world inspired in her. The solitude, for Anne, was immense. All that she saw, all that she felt was the tearing away

71

which separated her from what she saw and what she felt. The baneful clouds, if they covered the garden, nevertheless remained invisible in the huge cloud which enveloped them. The tree, a few steps away, was the tree with reference to which she was absent and distinct from everything. In all the souls which surrounded her like so many clearings, and which she could approach as intimately as her own soul, there was a silent, closed and desolate consciousness (the only light which made them perceptible), and it was solitude that created around her the sweet field of human contacts where, among infinite relationships full of harmony and tenderness, she saw her own mortal pain coming to meet her.

X

WHEN THEY FOUND HER stretched out on a bench in the garden, they thought she had fainted. But she had not fainted; she was sleeping, having entered into sleep by way of a repose deeper yet than sleep. Henceforth, her advance toward unconsciousness was a solemn combat in which she refused to give in to the thrill of drowsiness until she was wounded, dead already, and defended up to the last instant her right to consciousness and her share of clear thoughts. There was no complicity between her and the night. From the time the day started to fade, listening to the mysterious hymn which called her to another existence, she prepared herself for the struggle in which she could be defeated only by the total ruin of life. Her cheeks red, her eyes shining, calm and smiling, she enthusiastically mustered her strength. In vain the dusk brought its guilty song to her ear; in vain was a plot woven against her in favor of darkness. No sweetness penetrated her soul along the path of torpor, no semblance of the holiness which is acquired through the proper acceptance of illness. One felt that she would deliver into death nothing other than Anne, and that, fiercely intact, retaining everything that she was until the very end, she would not consent to save herself by any imaginary death from death itself. The night went on, and never had there been so sweet a night, so perfect to bend a sick person. The silence flowed, and the solitude full of friendship, the night full of hope, pressed upon Anne's stretched-out body. She lay awake, without delirium. There was no narcotic in the shadows, none of those suspicious touchings which permit the darkness to hypnotize those who resist sleep. The night acted nobly with Anne, and it was with the girl's own weapons, purity, confidence and peace, that it agreed to meet her. It was sweet, infinitely sweet in such a moment of great weakness to

75

feel around oneself a world so stripped of artifice and perfidiousness. How beautiful this night was, beautiful and not sweet, a classic night which fear did not render opaque, which put phantoms to flight and likewise wiped away the false beauty of the world. All that which Anne still loved, silence and solitude, were called night. All that which Anne hated, silence and solitude, were also called night. Absolute night where there were no longer any contradictory terms, where those who suffered were happy, where white found a common substance with black. And yet, night without confusion, without monsters, before which, without closing her eyes, she found her personal night, the one which her eyelids habitually created for her as they closed. Fully conscious, full of clarity, she felt her night join the night. She discovered herself in this huge exterior night in the core of her being, no longer needing to pass before a bitter and tormented soul to arrive at peace. She was sick, but how good this sickness was, this sickness which was not her own and which was the health of the world! How pure it was, this sleep which wrapped around her and which was not her own and blended with the supreme consciousness of all things! And Anne slept.

During the days which followed, she entered into a delicious field of peace, where to all eyes she appeared bathed in the intoxication of recovery. Before this magnificent spectacle, she too felt within herself this joy of the universe, but it was an icy joy. And she waited for that which could be neither a night nor a day to begin. Something came to her which was the prelude not to a recovery but to a surprising state of strength. No one understood that she was going to pass through the state of perfect health, through a marvelously balanced point of life, a pendulum swinging from one world to another. Through the

76

clouds which rushed over her head, she alone saw approaching with the speed of a shooting star the moment when, regaining contact with the earth, she would again grasp ordinary existence, would see nothing, feel nothing, when she could live, live finally, and perhaps even die, marvelous episode! She saw her very far away, this well Anne whom she did not know, through whom she was going to flow with a gay heart. Ah! Too dazzling instant! From the heart of the shadows a voice told her: Go.

Her real illness began. She no longer saw anyone but occasional friends, and those who still came stopped asking for news. Everyone understood that the treatment was not winning out over the illness. But Anne recognized in this another sort of scorn, and smiled at it. Whatever her fate might be, there was more life, more strength in her now than ever. Motionless for hours, sleeping with strength, speed, agility in her sleep, she was like an athlete who has remained prone for a long time, and her rest was like the rest of men who excel in running and wrestling. She finally conceived a strange feeling of pride in her body; she took a wonderful pleasure in her being; a serious dream made her feel that she was still alive, completely alive, and that she would have much more the feeling of being alive if she could wipe away the complacencies and the facile hopes. Mysterious moments during which, lacking all courage and incapable of movement, she seemed to be doing nothing, while, accomplishing an infinite task, she was incessantly climbing down to throw overboard the thoughts that belonged to her alive, the thoughts that belonged to her dead, to excavate within herself a refuge of extreme silence. Then the baneful stars appeared and she had to hurry: she gave up her last pleasures, got rid of her last sufferings.

What was uncertain was where she would come forth. She was already suffocating. My God, she is well; no, she is; she is perfect from the point of view of being; she has, elevated to the highest degree, the joy of the greatest spirit discovering his most beautiful thought. She is; no, she is well, she is slipping, the thunder of sensations falls upon her, she is smothered, she cries out, she hears herself, she lives. What joy! They give her something to drink, she cries, they console her. It is still night. Yet she could not help realizing it: around her, many things were changing, and a desolate climate surrounded her, as if gloomy spirits sought to draw her toward inhuman feelings. Slowly, by a pitiless protocol, they took from her the tenderness and friendship of the world. If she asked for the flowers she loved, they gave her artificial roses with no scent which, though they were the only beings more mortal than herself, did not reserve her the pleasure of wilting, fading and dying before her eyes. Her room became uninhabitable: given a northern exposure for the first time, with a single window which admitted only the late afternoon sun, deprived each day of another lovely object, this room gave every evidence of being secretly emptied in order to inspire in her the desire to leave it as soon as possible. The world too was devastated. They had exiled the pleasant seasons, asked the children to cry out in joy elsewhere, called into the street all the anger of cities, and it was an insurmountable wall of shattering sounds that separated her from mankind. Sometimes she opened her eyes and looked around with surprise: not only were things changing, but the beings most attached to her were changing as well. How could there be any doubt? There was a tragic lessening of tenderness for her. Henceforth her mother, plunged for hours on end in her armchair without a word, her face ashen,

78

carefully deprived of everything which might have made her lovable, no longer revealed anything of her affection but a feeling which made her ugly, at the very moment when Anne, as never before in her life, needed young and beautiful things. What she had once loved in her mother, gaity, laughter and tears, all the expressions of childhood repeated in an adult, all had disappeared from this face which expressed only fatigue, and it was only far away from this place that she could imagine her again capable of crying, of laughing—laughing, what a wonder! no one ever laughed here—a mother to everyone but her daughter. Anne raised her voice and asked her if she had been swimming. "Be quiet," said her mother. "Don't talk, you'll tire yourself." Obviously, there were no confidences to be shared with a person about to die, no possible relationship between her and those who are enjoying themselves, those who are alive. She sighed. And yet her mother resembled her, and what is more every day added a new trait to this resemblance. Contrary to the rule, it was the mother who took her daughter's face as a model, made it old, showed what it would be like at sixty. This obese Anne, whose eyes had turned gray as well as her hair, this was surely Anne if she were foolish enough to escape death. An innocent play: Anne was not duped. In spite of everything, life did not make itself hateful; she continued to love life. She was ready to die, but she was dying still loving flowers, even artificial flowers, feeling herself horribly orphaned in her death, passionately regretting this ugly Anne, this impotent Anne she would never become. Everything that was insidiously proposed to her so that she would not perceive that she was losing a great deal in leaving the world, this complicity of moralists and doctors, the traditional swindle perpetrated by

79

the sun and by men, offering on the last day as a last spectacle the ugliest images and faces in dark corners, where it is obvious that those who die are content to die . . . all these deceptions failed. Anne intended to pass into death completely alive, evading the intermediate states of disgust with life, refusal to live. Yet, surrounded by hardness, watched by her friends who tested her with an air of innocence, saying, "We can't come tomorrow, excuse us," and who then, after she had answered in true friendship, "That's not important, don't take any trouble," thought, "How insensitive she is becoming; she no longer cares about anything," faced with this sad plot to reduce her to feelings which, before dying, must degrade her and make all regrets superfluous, the time arrived when she saw herself betrayed by her discretion, her shyness, just what she retained of her habitual manner. Soon they would be saying, "She's no longer herself, it would be better if she died," and then: "What a deliverance for her if she died!" A gentle, irresistible pressure, how could one defend oneself against it? What did she have left that she could use to make it known that she had not changed? Just when she should have been throwing herself incessantly on her friends' shoulders, telling her doctor: "Save me, I don't want to die"—on that one condition they might still have considered her part of the world—she was greeting those who entered with a nod, giving them that which was most dear, a glance, a thought, pure impulses which just recently were still signs of true sympathy, but which now seemed the cold reserve of someone at odds with life at the very least. These scenes struck her and she understood that one does not ask restraint and delicacy of a person who is suffering, feelings which belong to healthy civilizations, but rather crudeness and frenzy. Since it was the law, since it was the only way to prove that she had never had so much attachment for all that surrounded her, she was seized by the desire to cry out, ready to make a move to reinforce every bond, ready to see in those near to her beings who were ever nearer. Unfortunately, it was too late: she no longer had the face or the body of her feelings, and she could no longer be gay with gaity. Now, to all those who came, whoever they might be (that was unimportant, time was short), she expressed by her closed eyes and her pinched lips the greatest passion ever experienced. And, not having enough affection to tell everyone how much she loved them, she had recourse as well to the hardest and coldest impulses of her soul. It was true that everything in her was hardening. Until then, she still had suffering. She suffered to open her eyes, suffered to receive the gentlest words: it was her one manner of being moved, and never had there been more sensitivity than in this glance which won the simple pleasure of seeing at the cost of cruel, tearing pain. But now, she hardly suffered any more at all; her body attained the ideal of egoism which is the ideal of every body: it was hardest at the moment of becoming weakest, a body which no longer cried out beneath the blows, borrowed nothing from the world, made itself, at the price of its beauty, the equivalent of a statue. This hardness weighed terribly on Anne; she felt the absence of all feeling in her as an immense void, and anguish clutched her. Then, in the form of this primordial passion, having now only a silent and dreary soul, a heart empty and dead, she offered her absence of friendship as the truest and purest friendship; she resigned herself, in this dark region where no one touched her, to responding to the ordinary affection of those around her by this supreme doubt concerning her being, by the desperate consciousness of being nothing any longer, by her anguish; she made the sacrifice, full of strangeness, of her certainty that she existed, in order to give a sense to this nothingness of love which she had become. And thus, deep within her, already sealed, already dead, the most profound passion came to be. To those who cried over her, cold and oblivious she returned hundredfold what they had given her, devoting to them the anticipation of her death, her death, the pure feeling, never purer, of her existence in the tortured anticipation of her nonexistence. She drew from herself not the weak emotions, sadness, regret, which were the lot of those around her, meaningless accidents with no chance of making any change in them, but the sole passion capable of threatening her very being, that which cannot be alienated and which would continue to burn when all the lights were put out. For the first time, she raised the words "give oneself" to their true meaning: she gave Anne, she gave much more than the life of Anne, she gave the ultimate gift, the death of Anne; she separated herself from her terribly strong feeling of being Anne, from the terribly anguished feeling of being Anne threatened with dying, and changed it into the yet more anguished feeling of being no longer Anne, but her mother, her mother threatened by death, the entire world on the point of annihilation. Never, within this body, this ideal of marble, monster of egoism, which had made of its unconsciousness the symbol of its estranged consciousness in a last pledge of friendship, never had there been more tenderness, and never within this poor being reduced to less than death, plundered of her most intimate treasure, her death, forced to die not personally but by the intermediary of all the others, had there been more being, more perfection of being. And so she had succeeded: her body was

82

truly the strongest, the happiest; this existence, so impoverished and restrained that it could not even receive its opposite, non-existence, was just what she was seeking. It was just that which permitted her to be equal, up to the very end, to all the others, in excellent form to disappear, full of strength for the last struggle. During the moments which followed, a strange fortress rose up around Anne. It did not resemble a city. There were no houses, no palace, no constructions of any sort; it was rather an immense sea, though the waters were invisible and the shore had disappeared. In this city, seated far from all things, sad last dream lost among the shadows, while the day faded and sobbing rose gently in the perspective of a strange horizon, Anne, like something which could not be represented, no longer a human being but simply a being, marvelously a being, among the mayflies and the falling suns, with the agonizing atoms, doomed species, wounded illnesses, ascended the course of waters where obscure origins floundered. She alas had no means of knowing where she arrived, but when the prolonged echoes of this enormous night were melting together into a dreary and vague uncon-sciousness, searching and wailing a wail which was like the tragic destruction of something nonliving, empty entities awoke and, like monsters constantly exchanging their absence of shape for other absences of shape and taming silence by terrible reminis-cences of silence, they went out in a mysterious agony. There is no way to express what they were, these shapes, beings, baneful entities—for us, can something which is not the day appear in the midst of the day, something which in an atmosphere of light and clarity would represent the shudder of terror which is the source of the day? But, insidiously, they made themselves recognized on the threshold of the irremediable as the obscure laws summoned to disappear with Anne. What was the result of this revelation? One would have said that everything was destroyed, but that everything was beginning again as well. Time, coming forth from its lakes, rolled her in an immense past, and, though she could not entirely leave space where she still breathed, drew her toward bottomless valleys where the world seemed to have returned to the moment of its creation. Anne's life—and this very word sounded like a defiant challenge in this place where there was no life—participated in the first ray thrown in all of eternity through the midst of indolent notions. Life-giving forces bathed her as if they had suddenly found in her breast, consecrated to death, the vainly sought meaning of the word "life-giving". Caprice, which built up the infinite framework of its combinations to conjure up the void, seized her and if she did not lose all existence at that moment, her discomfort was all the worse, her transformation greater than if, in her tranquil human state, she had actually abandoned life, for there was no absurdity she was allowed to escape, and in the interval of a time simulated by the fusion of eternity and the idea of nothingness, she became all the monsters in which creation tried itself in vain. Suddenly —and never was anything so abrupt—the failures of chance came to an end, and that which could in no way be expected received its success from a mysterious hand. Incredible moment, in which she reappeared in her own form, but accursed instant as well, for this unique combination, perceived in a flash, dissolved in a flash and the unshakeable laws which no shipwreck had been able to submerge were broken, giving in to a limitless caprice. An event so serious that no one near her perceived it and, although the atmosphere was heavy and weirdly transformed, no one felt the strangeness. The doctor bent over her and thought that she was dying according to the laws of death, not perceiving that she had already reached that instant when, in her, the laws were dying. She made an imperceptible motion; no one understood that she was floundering in the instant when death, destroying everything, might also destroy the possibility of annihilation. Alone, she saw the moment of the miracle coming, and she received no help. Oh, stupidity of those who are torn by grief! Beside her, as she was much less than dying, as she was dead, no one thought to multiply their absurd gestures, to liberate themselves from all convention and place themselves in the condition of primal creation. No one sought out the false beings, the hypocrites, the equivocal beings, all those who jeer at the idea of reason. No one said in the silence: "Let us hurry and before she is cold let us thrust her into the unknown. Let us create a darkness about her so that the law may abandon itself disloyally to the impossible. And ourselves, let us go away, lose all hope: hope itself must be forgotten."

Now Anne opened her eyes. There was in fact no more hope. This moment of supreme distraction, this trap into which those who have nearly vanquished death fall, ultimate return of Eurydice, in looking one last time toward the visible, Anne had just fallen into it as well. She opened her eyes without the least curiosity, with the lassitude of someone who knows perfectly well in advance what will be offered to her sight. Yes, there is her room, there is her mother, her friend Louise, there is Thomas. My God, that was just what it was. All those she loved were there. Her death must absolutely have the character of a solemn farewell, each one must receive his squeeze of the hand, his smile. And it is true that she squeezed their hands, smiled at them, loved them. She breathed gently. She had her face turned toward them as if she wished to see them up to the very last moment. Everything that had to be done, she did it. Like every dying person, she went away observing the rituals, pardoning her enemies, loving her friends, without admitting the secret which no one admits: that all this was already insignificant. Already she had no more importance. She looked at them with an ever more modest look, a simple look, which for them, for humans, was an empty look. She squeezed their hands ever more gently, with a grip which did not leave a trace, a grip which they could not feel. She did not speak. These last moments must be without any memory. Her face, her shoulders must become invisible, as is proper for something which is fading away. Her mother whined: "Anne, do you recognize me? Answer me, squeeze my hand." Anne heard this voice: what good was it, her mother was no longer anything more than an insignificant being. She also heard Thomas; in fact, she knew now what she had to say to Thomas, she knew exactly the words she had searched for all her life in order to reach him. But she remained silent; she thought: what good is it—and this word was also the word she was seeking—Thomas is insignificant. Let us sleep.

XI

WHEN ANNE HAD DIED, Thomas did not leave the room, and he seemed deeply afflicted. This grief caused great discomfort to all those present, and they had the premonition that what he was saying to himself at that moment was the prelude to a drama the thought of which filled them with consternation. They went away sadly, and he remained alone. One might think that what he was saying to himself could in no way allow itself to be read, but he took care to speak as if his words had a chance of being heard and he left aside the strange truth to which he seemed chained.

"I suspected," he said, "that Anne had premeditated her death. This evening she was peaceful and noble. Without the coquettishness which hides from the dead their true state, without that last cowardice which makes them wait to die by the doctor's hand, she bestowed death upon herself, entirely, in an instant. I approached this perfect corpse. The eyes had closed. The mouth did not smile. There was not a single reflection of life in the face. A body without consolation, she did not hear the voice which asked, 'Is it possible?' and no one dreamed of saying of her what is said of the dead who lack courage, what Christ said of the girl who was not worthy of burial, to humiliate her: she is sleeping. She was not sleeping. She was not changed, either. She had stopped at the point where she resembled only herself, and where her face, having only Anne's expression, was disturbing to look at. I took her hand. I placed my lips on her forehead. I treated her as if she were alive and, because she was unique among the dead in still having a face and a hand, my gestures did not seem insane. Did she appear alive, then? Alas, all that prevented her from being distinguished from a real person was that which verified her annihilation. She was entirely within

89

herself: in death, abounding in life. She seemed more weighty, more in control of herself. No Anne was lacking in the corpse of Anne. All the Annes had been necessary to bring her back to nothing. The jealous, the pensive, the violent, had served only once, to make her completely dead. At her end, she seemed to need more being to be annihilated than to be, and, dead precisely from this excess which permitted her to show herself entirely, she bestowed on death all the reality and all the existence which constituted the proof of her own nothingness. Neither impalpable nor dissolved in the shadows, she imposed herself ever more strongly on the senses. As her death became more real, she grew, she became larger, she hollowed out a deep tomb in her couch. Obliterated as she was, she drew every glance to her. We who remained beside her, we felt ourselves compressed by this huge being. We were suffocating for lack of air. Each of us discovered with anguish what only casket-bearers know, that the dead double in weight, that they are the largest, the most powerful of all beings. Each bore his portion of this manifest dead person. Her mother, seeing her so like a living person, naively lifted up the girl's head and was unable to bear the enormous weight, proof of the destruction of her daughter. And then, I stayed alone with her. She had surely died for that moment when people might think she had defeated me. For dying had been her ruse to deliver a body into nothingness. At the moment everything was being destroyed she had created that which was most difficult: she had not drawn something out of nothing (a meaningless act), but given to nothing, in its form of nothing, the form of something. The act of not seeing had now its integral eye. The silence, the real silence, the one which is not composed of silenced words, of possible thoughts, had a voice.

Her face, more beautiful from one instant to the next, was constructing her absence. There was not a single part of her which was still the prop of any sort of reality. It was then, when her story and the story of her death had faded away together and there was no one left in the world to name Anne, that she attained the moment of immortality in nothingness, in which what has ceased to be enters into a thoughtless dream. It was truly night. I was surrounded by stars. The totality of things wrapped about me and I prepared myself for the agony with the exalted consciousness that I was unable to die. But, at that instant, what she alone had perceived up until then appeared manifest to everyone: I revealed to them, in me, the strangeness of their condition and the shame of an endless existence. Of course I could die, but death shone forth perfidiously for me as the death of death, so that, becoming the eternal man taking the place of the moribund, this man without crime, without any reason for dying who is every man who dies, I would die, a dead person so alien to death that I would spend my supreme moment in a time when it was already impossible to die and yet I would live all the hours of my life in the hour in which I could no longer live them. Who more than I was deprived of the last moment full of hope, so totally deprived of the last consolation which memory offers to those who despair, to those who have forgotten happiness and toss themselves from the pinnacle of life in order to recall its joys? And yet I was really a dead person, I was even the only possible dead person, I was the only man who did not give the impression that he died by chance. All my strength, the sense I had, in taking the hemlock, of being not Socrates dying but Socrates increasing himself through Plato, this certainty of being unable to disappear which belongs only to beings afflicted with a terminal illness, this serenity before the scaffold which bestows upon the condemned their true pardon, made of every instant of my life the instant in which I was going to leave life. All my being seemed to mingle with death. As naturally as men believe they are alive, accepting as an inevitable impulse their breathing, the circulation of their blood, so I ceased living. I drew my death from my very existence, and not from the absence of existence. I presented a dead person who did not confine himself to the appearance of a diminished being, and this dead person, filled with passions but insensitive, calling for his thought upon an absence of thought and yet carefully separating out whatever there might be in it of void, of negation in life, in order not to make of his death a metaphor, an even weaker image of normal death, brought to its highest point the paradox and the impossibility of death. What then distinguished me from the living? Just this, that neither night, nor loss of consciousness, nor indifference called me from life. And what distinguished me from the dead, unless it was a personal act in which at every instant, going beyond appearances which are generally sufficient, I had to find the sense and the definitive explanation of my death? People did not want to believe it, but my death was the same thing as death. Before men who know only how to die, who live up until the end, living people touched by the end of their lives as if by a slight accident, I had only death as an anthropometric index. This is in fact what made my destiny inexplicable. Under the name Thomas, in this chosen state in which I might be named and described, I had the appearance of any living person, but since I was real only under the name of death, I let the baneful spirit of the shadows show through, blood mixed with my blood, and the mirror of each of my days reflected the confused images of death and life. And so my fate stupefied the crowd. This Thomas forced me to appear, while I was living, not even the eternal dead person I was and on which no one could fix their glance, but an ordinary dead person, a body without life, an insensitive sensitivity, thought without thought. At the highest point of contradiction, I was this illegitimate dead person. Represented in my feelings by a double for whom each feeling was as absurd as for a dead person, at the pinnacle of passion I attained the pinnacle of estrangement, and I seemed to have been removed from the human condition because I had truly accomplished it. Since, in each human act, I was the dead person that at once renders it possible and impossible and, if I walked, if I thought, I was the one whose complete absence alone makes the step or the thought possible, before the beasts, beings who do not bear within them their dead double, I lost my last reason for existing. There was a tragic distance between us. A man without a trace of animal nature, I ceased to be able to express myself with my voice which no longer sang, no longer even spoke as the voice of a talking bird speaks. I thought, outside of all image and all thought, in an act which consisted of being unthinkable. Every moment, I was this purely human man, supreme individual and unique example, with whom, in dying, each person makes an exchange, and who dies alone in place of all. With me, the species died each time, completely. Whereas, if these composite beings called men had been left to die on their own, they would have been seen to survive miserably in pieces divided up among different things, reconstituted in a mixture of insect, tree and earth, I disappeared without a trace and fulfilled my role as the one, the unique dead person to perfection. I was thus the sole corpse of humanity. In contradiction of those who say that humanity does not die, I proved in every way that only humanity is capable of dying. I appeared in every one of these poor moribunds, ugly as they were, at the instant full of beauty in which, renouncing all their links with the other species, they become, by renouncing not only the world, but the jackal, the ivy, they become uniquely men. These scenes still glow within me like magnificent festivals. I approached them and their anxiety grew. These miserable creatures who were becoming men felt the same terror at feeling themselves men as Isaac on the altar at becoming a lamb. None of them recognized my presence and yet there was in the depths of them, like a fatal ideal, a void which exerted a temptation over them, which they felt as a person of such complete and imposing reality that they had to prefer that person to any other, even at the cost of their existence. Then the gates of agony opened and they flung themselves into their error. They shrunk, forced themselves to be reduced to nothing to correspond to this model of nothingness which they took for the model of life. They loved only life and they struggled against it. They perished from a taste for life so strong that life seemed to them that death whose approach they anticipated, which they thought they were fleeing as they hurled themselves forward to meet it and which they recognized only at the very last moment when, as the voice was saying to them, 'It is too late,' I was already taking their place. What happened then? When the guard who had stepped away returned, he saw someone who resembled no one, a faceless stranger, the very opposite of a being. And the most loving friend, the best son saw their senses altered before this alien shape and cast a look of horror on that which they loved the most, a cold, unrecognizable look as if death had taken not their friend but their feelings, and now they were the ones, they, the living, who were changing so profoundly that it might have been called a death. Even their relations among themselves were altered. If they touched one another it was with a shudder, feeling that they were experiencing contact with a stranger. Each, with reference to the other, in complete solitude, complete intimacy, each became for the other the only dead person, the only survivor. And when he who wept and he who was wept over came to blend together, became one, then there came an outburst of despair, this strangest moment of the mourning, when, in the mortuary chamber, friends and relations add to themselves the one who has left their number, feel themselves of the same substance, as respectable as he, and even consider themselves the authentic dead person, the only one worthy to impose upon their common grief. And everything, then, seems simple to them. They again bestow on the dead person his familiar nature, after having brushed past him as if he were a scandalous reality. They say: 'I never understood my poor husband (my poor father) better.' They imagine they understand him, not only such as he was when living, but dead, having the same knowledge of him that a vigorous tree has of a cut branch, by the sap which still flows. Then, gradually, the living assimilate those who have disappeared completely. Pondering the dead in pondering oneself becomes the formula of appeasement. They are seen entering triumphally into existence. The cemeteries are emptied. The sepulchral absence again becomes invisible. The strange contradictions vanish. And it is in a harmonious world that everyone goes on living, immortal to the end.

"The certainty of dying, the certainty of not dying, there is all that is left, for the crowd, of the reality of death. But those who contemplated me felt that death could also associate with existence and form this decisive word: death exists. They have developed the habit of saying about existence everything they could say of death for me and, rather than murmur, 'I am, I am not,' mix the terms together in a single happy combination and say, 'I am, while I am not,' and likewise, 'I am not, while I am,' without there being the slightest attempt to force contradictory words together, rubbing them one against the other like stones. As voices were called down upon my existence, affirming in succession, with equal passion: 'He exists for always, he does not exist for always,' that existence took on a fatal character in their eyes. It seemed that I was walking comfortably over the abysses and that, complete in myself, not half-phantom half-man, I penetrated my perfect nothingness. A sort of integral ventriloquist, wherever I cried out, that is where I was not, and also just where I was, being in every way the equivalent of silence. My word, as if composed of excessively high vibrations, first devoured silence, then the word. I spoke, I was by that act immediately placed in the center of the intrigue. I threw myself into the pure fire which consumed me at the same time it made me visible. I became transparent before my own sight. Look at men: the pure void summons their eye to call itself blind and a perpetual alibi exchanged between the night outside and the night within permits them to retain the illusion of day throughout their lives. For me, it was this very illusion which by an inexplicable act seemed to have issued from myself. I found myself with two faces, glued one to the other. I was in constant contact with two shores. With one hand showing that I was indeed there, with the other—what am I saying?—without the other, with this body which, imposed on my real body, depended entirely on a negation of the body, I entered into absolute dispute with myself. Having two eyes, one of which was possessed of extreme visual acuity, it was with the other which was an eye only because of its refusal to see that I saw everything visible. And so on, for all my organs. I had a part of myself submerged, and it was to this part, lost in a constant shipwreck, that I owed my direction, my face, my necessity. I found my proof in this movement toward the nonexistent in which the proof that I existed, rather than becoming degraded, was reinforced to the point of becoming manifestly true. I made a supreme effort to keep outside myself, as near as possible to the place of beginnings. Now, far from achieving as a complete man, as an adolescent, as protoplasm, the state of the possible, I made my way toward something complete, and I caught a glimpse in these depths of the strange face of him who I really was and who had nothing in common with an already dead man or with a man yet to be born: a marvelous companion with whom I wished with all my might to blend myself, yet separate from me, with no path that might lead me to him. How could I reach him? By killing myself: absurd plan. Between this corpse, the same as a living person but without life, and this unnameable, the same as a dead person but without death, I could not see a single line of relationship. No poison might unite me with that which could bear no name, could not be designated by the opposite of its opposite, nor conceived in relationship to anything. Death was a crude metamorphosis beside the indiscernible nullity which I nevertheless coupled with the name Thomas. Was it then a fantasy, this enigma, the creation of a word maliciously formed to destroy all words? But if I advanced within myself, hurrying laboriously toward my precise noon, I yet experienced

as a tragic certainty, at the center of the living Thomas, the inaccessible proximity of that Thomas which was nothingness, and
the more the shadow of my thought shrunk, the more I conceived of myself in this faultless clarity as the possible, the will-
ing host of this obscure Thomas. In the plentitude of my reality,
I believed I was reaching the unreal. O my consciousness, it was
not a question of imputing to you—in the form of revery, of
fainting away, of hiatus—that which, having been unable to be
assimilated to death, should have passed for something worse,
your own death. What am I saying? I felt this nothingness
bound to your extreme existence as an unexceptionable condition. I felt that between it and you undeniable ratios were being
established. All the logical couplings were incapable of expressing this union in which, without *then* or *because*, you came together, both cause and effect at once, unreconcilable and indis-
soluble. Was it your opposite? No, I said not. But it seemed that
if, slightly falsifying the relationships of words, I had sought the
opposite of your opposite, having lost my true path I would
have arrived, without turning back, proceeding wondrously
from you-consciousness (at once existence and life) to you-un-
consciousness (at once reality and death), I would have arrived,
setting out into the terrible unknown, at an image of my enigma
which would have been at once nothingness and existence. And
with these two words I would have been able to destroy, incessantly, that which was signified by the one by that which was
signified by the other, and by that which the two signified, and
at the same time I would have destroyed by their oppositeness
that which constituted the oppositeness of these two opposites,
and I would have finished, kneading them endlessly to melt that
which was untouchable, by reemerging right beside myself,

Harpagon suddenly catching his thief and grabbing hold of his own arm. It was then that, deep within a cave, the madness of the taciturn thinker appeared before me and unintelligible words rung in my ears while I wrote on the wall these sweet words: 'I think, therefore I am not.' These words brought me a delicious vision. In the midst of an immense countryside, a flaming lens received the dispersed rays of the sun and, by those fires, became conscious of itself as a monstrous I, not at the points at which it received them, but at the point at which it projected and united them in a single beam. At this focus-point, the center of a terrible heat, it was wondrously active, it illuminated, it burned, it devoured; the entire universe became a flame at the point at which the lens touched it; and the lens did not leave it until it was destroyed. Nevertheless, I perceived that this mirror was like a living animal consumed by its own fire. The earth it set ablaze was its entire body reduced to dust, and, from this unceasing flame, it drew, in a torrent of sulphur and gold, the consequence that it was constantly annihilated. It began to speak and its voice seemed to come from the bottom of my heart. I think, it said, I bring together all that which is light without heat, rays without brilliance, unrefined products; I brew them together and conjugate them, and, in a primary absence of myself, I discover myself as a perfect unity at the point of greatest intensity. I think, it said, I am subject and object of an all-powerful radiation; a sun using all its energy to make itself night, as well as to make itself sun. I think: there at the point where thought joins with me I am able to subtract myself from being, without diminishing, without changing, by means of a metamorphosis which saves me for myself, beyond any point of reference from which I might be seized. It is the property of my thought, not to assure

99

me of existence (as all things do, as a stone does), but to assure me of being in nothingness itself, and to invite me not to be, in order to make me feel my marvelous absence. I think, said Thomas, and this invisible, inexpressible, nonexistent Thomas I became meant that henceforth I was never there where I was, and there was not even anything mysterious about it. My existence became entirely that of an absent person who, in every act I performed, produced the same act and did not perform it. I walked, counting my steps, and my life was that of a man cast in concrete, with no legs, with not even the idea of movement. Beneath the sun, the one man the sun did not illuminate went forward, and this light which hid from itself, this torrid heat which was not heat, nevertheless issued from a real sun. I looked before me: a girl was sitting on a bench, I approached, I sat down beside her. There was only a slight distance between us. Even when she turned her head away, she perceived me entirely. She saw me with my eyes which she exchanged for her own, with my face which was practically her face, with my head which sat easily on her shoulders. She was already joining herself to me. In a single glance, she melted in me and in this intimacy discovered my absence. I felt she was oppressed, trembling. I imagined her hand ready to approach me, to touch me, but the only hand she would have wanted to take was ungraspable. I understood that she was passionately searching out the cause of her discomfort, and when she saw that there was nothing abnormal about me she was seized with terror. I was like her. My strangeness had as its cause all that which made me not seem strange to her. With horror she discovered in everything that was ordinary about her the source of everything that was extraordinary about me. I was her tragic double. If she got up, she knew, watching me get up, that it was an impossible movement, but she also knew that it was a very simple movement for her, and her fright reached a peak of intensity because there was no difference between us. I lifted my hand to my forehead, it was warm, I smoothed my hair. She looked at me with great pity. She had pity for this man with no head, with no arms, completely absent from the summer and wiping away his perspiration at the cost of unimaginable effort. Then she looked at me again and vertigo seized her. For what was there that was insane in my action? It was something absurd which nothing explained, nothing designated, the absurdity of which destroyed itself, absurdity of being absurd, and in every way like something reasonable. I offered this girl the experience of something absurd, and it was a terrible test. I was absurd, not because of the goat's foot which permitted me to walk with a human pace, but because of my regular anatomy, my complete musculature which permitted me a normal pace, nevertheless an absurd pace, and, normal as it was, more and more absurd. Then, in turn, I looked at her: I brought her the one true mystery, which consisted of the absence of mystery, and which she could therefore do nothing but search for, eternally. Everything was clear in me, everything was simple: there was no other side to the pure enigma. I showed her a face with no secret, indecipherable; she read in my heart as she had never read in any other heart; she knew why I had been born, why I was there, and the more she reduced the element of the unknown in me, the more her discomfort and her fright increased. She was forced to divulge me, she separated me from my last shadows, in the fear of seeing me with no shadow. She pursued this mystery desperately; she destroyed me insatiably. Where was I for her? I had disappeared and I felt her gathering herself up to throw herself into my absence as if into her mirror. There henceforth was her reflection, her exact shape, there was her personal abyss. She saw herself and desired herself, she obliterated herself and rejected herself, she had ineffable doubts about herself, she gave in to the temptation of meeting herself there where she was not. I saw her giving in. I put my hand on her knees.

"I am sad; the evening is coming. But I also experience the opposite of sadness. I am at that point where it is sufficient to experience a little melancholy to feel hate and joy. I feel that I am tender, not only toward men but toward their passions. I love them, loving the feelings by which one might have loved them. I bring them devotion and life at the second degree: to separate us there is nothing more than that which would have united us, friendship, love. In the depths of myself, at the end of the day, strange emotions are deposited which take me for their object. I love myself with the spirit of revulsion, I calm myself with fear, I taste life in the feeling which separates me from it. All these passions, forced within me, produce nothing other than that which I am and the entire universe exhausts its rage to make me feel something, vaguely, of myself, feel some being which does not feel itself. Now calm comes down with the night. I can no longer name a single feeling. If I were to call my present state impassivity, I could just as well call it fire. What I feel is the source of that which is felt, the origin believed to be without feeling, the indiscernible impulse of enjoyment and revulsion. And, it is true, I feel nothing. I am reaching regions where that which one experiences has no relation with that which is experienced. I go down into the hard block of marble with the sensation of slipping into the sea. I drown myself in mute bronze. Everywhere hardness, diamond, pitiless fire, and yet the sensation is that of foam. Absolute absence of desire. No movement, no phantom of movement, neither anything immobile. It is in such great poverty, such absence, that I recognize all the passions from which I have been withdrawn by an insignificant miracle. Absent from Anne, absent from my love for Anne to the extent that I loved Anne. And absent, doubly, from myself, carried each time by desire beyond desire and destroying even this nonexistent Thomas where I felt I truly existed. Absent from this absence, I back away infinitely. I lose all contact with the horizon I am fleeing. I flee my flight. Where is the end? Already the void seems to me the ultimate in fullness: I understood it, I experienced it, I exhausted it. Now I am like a beast terrified by its own leap. I am falling in horror of my fall. I aspire vertiginously to reject myself from myself. Is it night? Have I come back, another, to the place where I was? Again there is a supreme moment of calm. Silence, refuge of transparency for the soul. I am terrified by this peace. I experience a sweetness which contains me for a moment and consumes me. If I had a body, I would grip my throat with my hands. I would like to suffer. I would like to prepare a simple death for myself, in an agony in which I would tear myself to pieces. What peace! I am ravaged by delights. There is no longer anything of me which does not open itself to this future void as if to a frightful enjoyment. No notion, no image, no feeling sustains me. Whereas just a moment ago I felt nothing, simply experiencing each feeling as a great absence, now in the complete absence of feelings I experience the strongest feeling. I draw my fright from the fright which I do not have. Fright, terror, the metamorphosis passes all thought. I am at grips with a feeling which reveals to me that I cannot experience it, and it is at that moment that I experience it with a force which makes it an inexpressible torment. And that is nothing, for I could experience it as something other than what it is, fright experienced as enjoyment. But the horror is that there emerges within it the consciousness that no feeling is possible, and likewise no thought and no consciousness. And the worst horror is that in apprehending it, far from dissipating it like a phantom by touching it, I cause it to increase beyond measure. I experience it as not experiencing it and as experiencing nothing, being nothing, and this absurdity is its monstrous substance. Something totally absurd serves as my reason. I feel myself dead—no; I feel myself, living, infinitely more dead than dead. I discover my being in the vertiginous abyss where it is not, an absence, an absence where it sets itself like a god. I am not and I endure. An inexorable future stretches forth infinitely for this suppressed being. Hope turns in fear against time which drags it forward. All feelings gush out of themselves and come together, destroyed, abolished, in this feeling which molds me, makes me and unmakes me, causes me to feel, hideously, in a total absence of feeling, my reality in the shape of nothingness. A feeling which has to be given a name and which I call anguish. Here is the night. The darkness hides nothing. My first perception is that this night is not a provisional absence of light. Far from being a possible locus of images, it is composed of all that which is not seen and is not heard, and, listening to it, even a man would know that, if he were not a man, he would hear nothing. In true night, then, the unheard, the invisible are lacking, all those things that make the night habitable. It does not allow anything other than itself to be attributed to it; it is impenetrable. I am truly in the beyond, if the beyond is that which admits of no beyond. Along with the feeling that everything has vanished, this night brings me the feeling that everything is near me. It is the supreme relationship which is sufficient unto itself; it leads me eternally to itself, and an obscure race from the identical to the identical imparts to me the desire of a wonderful progress. In this absolute repetition of the same is born true movement which cannot lead to rest. I feel myself directed by the night toward the night. A sort of being, composed of all that which is excluded from being, presents itself as the goal of my undertaking. That which is not seen, is not understood, is not, creates right beside me the level of another night, and yet the same, toward which I aspire unspeakably, though I am already mingled with it. Within my reach there is a world—I call it world, as, dead, I would call the earth nothingness. I call it world because there is no other possible world for me. Just as when one moves toward an object, I believe I am making it come closer, but *it* is the one that understands *me*. Invisible and outside of being, it perceives me and sustains me in being. Itself, I perceive it, an unjustifiable chimera if I were not there, I perceive it, not in the vision I have of it, but in the vision and the knowledge it has of me. I am seen. Beneath this glance, I commit myself to a passivity which, rather than diminishing me, makes me real. I seek neither to distinguish it, nor to attain it, nor to suppose it. Perfectly negligent, by my distraction I retain for it the quality of inaccessibility which is appropriate to it. My senses, my imagination, my spirit, all are dead on the side on which it looks at me. I seize it as the sole necessity, that which is not even a hypothesis . . . as my sole resistance, I who am annihilating myself. I am seen. Porous, identical to the night, which is not seen, I am seen.

Being as imperceptible as it is, I know it as it sees me. It is even the last possibility I have of being seen, now that I no longer exist. It is that glance which continues to see me in my absence. It is the eye that my disappearance requires more and more as it becomes more complete, to perpetuate me as an object of vision. In the night we are inseparable. Our intimacy is this very night. Any distance between us is suppressed, but suppressed in order that we may not come closer one to the other. It is a friend to me, a friendship which divides us. It is united with me, a union which distinguishes us. It is myself, I who do not exist for myself. In this instant, I have no existence except for it, which exists only for me. My being subsists only from a supreme point of view which is precisely incompatible with my point of view. The perspective in which I fade away for my eyes restores me as a complete image for the unreal eye to which I deny all images. A complete image with reference to a world devoid of image which imagines me in the absence of any imaginable figure. The being of a nonbeing of which I am the infinitely small negation which it instigates as its profound harmony. In the night shall I become the universe? I feel that in every part of me, invisible and nonexistent, I am supremely, totally visible. Marvelously bound, I offer in a single unique image the expression of the world. Without color, inscribed in no thinkable form, neither the product of a powerful brain, I am the sole necessary image. On the retina of the absolute eye, I am the tiny inverted image of all things. In my scale, I bestow upon it the personal vision not only of the sea, but of the hillside still ringing with the cry of the first man. There, everything is distinct, everything is melted together. To the prism that I am, a perfect unity restores the infinite dissipation which makes it possible to see everything without seeing anything. I renew the crude undertaking of Noah. I enclose within my absence the principle of totality which is real and perceptible only for the absurd being who overflows totality, for that absurd spectator who examines me, loves me and draws me powerfully into his absurdity. To the extent that I contain within me that whole to which I offer (as the water offered Narcissus) the reflection in which it desires itself, I am excluded from the whole and the whole itself is excluded therefrom, and yet more is the prodigious one who is absent excluded, absent from me and from everything, absent for me as well, and yet for whom I work alone at this absurdity which he accepts. All of us are condemned by the same logical proscription, all three of us (a number which is monstrous when one of the three is everything). We are united by the mutual check in which we hold each other, with this difference, that it is only with reference to my contemplator that I am the irrational being, representing everything outside of him, but it is also with reference to him that I cannot be irrational, if he himself represents the reason of this existence outside of everything. Now, in this night, I come forward bearing everything, toward that which infinitely exceeds everything. I progress beyond the totality which I nevertheless tightly embrace. I go on the margins of the universe, boldly walking elsewhere than where I can be, and a little outside of my steps. This slight extravagance, this deviation toward that which cannot be, is not only my own impulse leading me to a personal madness, but the impulse of the reason which I bear with me. With me the laws gravitate outside the laws, the possible outside the possible. O night, now nothing will make me be, nothing will separate me from you. I adhere marvelously to the simplicity to which you invite me.

I lean over you, your equal, offering you a mirror for your perfect nothingness, for your shadows which are neither light nor absence of light, for this void which contemplates. To all that which you are, and, for our language, are not, I add a consciousness. I make you experience your supreme identity as a relationship, I name you and define you. You become a delicious passivity. You attain entire possession of yourself in abstention. You give to the infinite the glorious feeling of its limits. O night, I make you taste your ecstasy. I perceive in myself the second night which brings you the consciousness of your barrenness. You bloom into new restrictions. By my mediation, you contemplate yourself eternally. I am with you, as if you were my creation. My creation. . . . What strange light is this which falls upon me? Could the effort to expel myself from every created thing have made of me the supreme creator? Having stretched all my strength against being, I find myself again at the heart of creation. Myself, working against the act of creating, I have made myself the creator. Here I am, conscious of the absolute as of an object I am creating at the same time I am struggling not to create myself. That which has never had any principle admits me at its eternal beginning, I who am the stubborn refusal of my own beginning. It is I, the origin of that which has no origin. I create that which cannot be created. Through an all-powerful ambiguity, the uncreated is the same word for it and for me. For it, I am the image of what it would be, if it did not exist. Since it is not possible that it should exist, by my absurdity I am its sovereign reason. I force it to exist. O night, I am itself. Here it has drawn me into the trap of its creation. And now it is the one that forces me to exist. And I am the one who is its eternal prisoner. It creates me for itself alone. It makes me, nothingness that I am, like unto nothingness. In a cowardly way it delivers me to joy."

XII

THOMAS WENT OUT into the country and saw that spring was beginning. In the distance, ponds spread forth their murky waters, the sky was dazzling, life was young and free. When the sun climbed on the horizon, the genera, the races, even the species of the future, represented by individuals with no species, peopled the solitude in a disorder full of splendor. Dragonflies without wing-cases, which should not have flown for ten million years, tried to take flight; blind toads crawled through the mud trying to open their eyes which were capable of vision only in the future. Others, drawing attention to themselves through the transparency of time, forced whoever looked at them to become a visionary by a supreme prophecy of the eye. A dazzling light in which, illuminated, impregnated by the sun, everything was in movement to receive the glint of the new flames. The idea of perishing pushed the chrysalis to become a butterfly; death for the green caterpillar consisted of receiving the dark wings of the sphinx moth, and there was a proud and defiant consciousness in the mayflies which gave the intoxicating impression that life would go on forever. Could the world be more beautiful? The ideal of color spread out across the fields. Across the transparent and empty sky extended the ideal of light. The fruitless trees, the flowerless flowers bore freshness and youth at the tips of their stems. In place of the rose, the rose-bush bore a black flower which could not wilt. The spring enveloped Thomas like a sparkling night and he felt himself called softly by this nature overflowing with joy. For him, an orchard bloomed at the center of the earth, birds flew in the nothingness and an immense sea spread out at his feet. He walked. Was it the new brilliance of the light? It seemed that, through a phenomenon awaited for centuries, the earth now saw him. The primroses

113

allowed themselves to be viewed by his glance which did not see. The cuckoo began its unheard song for his deaf ear. The universe contemplated him. The magpie he awoke was already no more than a universal bird which cried out for the profaned world. A stone rolled, and it slipped through an infinity of metamorphoses the unity of which was that of the world in its splendor. In the midst of these tremblings, solitude burst forth. Against the depths of the sky a radiant and jealous face was seen to rise up, whose eyes absorbed all other faces. A sound began, deep and harmonious, ringing inside the bells like the sound no one can hear. Thomas went forward. The great misfortune which was to come still seemed a gentle and tranquil event. In the valleys, on the hills, his passing spread out like a dream on the shining earth. It was strange to pass through a perfumed spring which held back its scents, to contemplate flowers which, with their dazzling colors, could not be perceived. Birds splashed with color, chosen to be the repertory of shades, rose up, presenting red and black to the void. Drab birds, designated to be the conservatory of music without notes, sang the absence of song. A few mayflies were still seen flying with real wings, because they were going to die, and that was all. Thomas went his way and, suddenly, the world ceased to hear the great cry which crossed the abysses. A lark, heard by no one, tossed forth shrill notes for a sun it did not see and abandoned air and space, not finding in nothingness the pinnacle of its ascent. A rose which bloomed as he passed touched Thomas with the brilliance of its thousand corollas. A nightingale that followed him from tree to tree made its extraordinary mute voice heard, a singer mute for itself and for all others and nevertheless singing the magnificent song. Thomas went forward toward the city. There was no longer sound or silence. The man immersed in the waves piled up by the absence of flood spoke to his horse in a dialogue consisting of a single voice. The city which spoke to itself in a dazzling monologue of a thousand voices rested in the debris of illuminated and transparent images. Where, then, was the city? Thomas, at the heart of the agglomeration, met no one. The enormous buildings with their thousands of inhabitants were deserted, deprived of that primordial inhabitant who is the architect powerfully imprisoned in the stone. Immense unbuilt cities. The buildings were piled one on the other. Clusters of edifices and monuments accumulated at the intersections. Out to the horizon, inaccessible shores of stone were seen rising slowly, impasses which led to the cadaverous apparition of the sun. This somber contemplation could not go on. Thousands of men, nomads in their homes, living nowhere, stretched out to the limits of the world. They threw themselves, buried themselves in the earth where, walled between bricks carefully cemented by Thomas, while the enormous mass of things was smashed beneath a cloud of ashes, they went forward, dragging the immensity of space beneath their feet. Mingling with the rough beginnings of creation, for an infinitely small time they piled up mountains. They rose up as stars, ravaging the universal order with their random course. With their blind hands, they touched the invisible worlds to destroy them. Suns which no longer shone bloomed in their orbits. The great day embraced them in vain. Thomas still went forward. Like a shepherd he led the flock of the constellations, the tide of star-men toward the first night. Their procession was solemn and noble, but toward what end, and in what form? They thought they were still captives within a soul whose borders they wished to cross.

Memory seemed to them that desert of ice which a magnificent sun was melting and in which they seized again, by somber and cold remembering, separated from the heart which had cherished it, the world in which they were trying to live again. Though they no longer had bodies, they enjoyed having all the images representing a body, and their spirit sustained the infinite procession of imaginary corpses. But little by little forgetfulness came. Monstrous memory, in which they rushed about in frightful intrigues, folded upon them and chased them from this fortress where they still seemed, feebly, to breathe. A second time they lost their bodies. Some who proudly plunged their glance into the sea, others who clung with determination to their name, lost the memory of speech, while they repeated Thomas's empty word. Memory was wiped away and, as they became the accursed fever which vainly flattered their hopes, like prisoners with only their chains to help them escape, they tried to climb back up to the life they could not imagine. They were seen leaping desperately out of their enclosure, floating, secretly slipping forward, but when they thought they were on the very point of victory, trying to build out of the absence of thought a stronger thought which would devour laws, theorems, wisdom . . . then the guardian of the impossible seized them, and they were engulfed in the shipwreck. A prolonged, heavy fall: had they come, as they dreamed, to the confines of the soul they thought they were traversing? Slowly they came out of this dream and discovered a solitude so great that when the monsters which had terrified them when they were men came near them, they looked on them with indifference, saw nothing, and, leaning over the crypt, remained there in a profound inertia, waiting mysteriously for the tongue whose birth every prophet has felt deep in his throat to come forth from the sea and force the impossible words into their mouths. This waiting was a sinister mist exhaled drop by drop from the summit of a mountain; it seemed it could never end. But when, from the deepest of the shadows there rose up a prolonged cry which was like the end of a dream, they all recognized the ocean, and they perceived a glance whose immensity and sweetness awoke in them unbearable desires. Becoming men again for an instant, they saw in the infinite an image they grasped and, giving in to a last temptation, they stripped themselves voluptuously in the water.

Thomas as well watched this flood of crude images, and then, when it was his turn, he threw himself into it, but sadly, desperately, as if the shame had begun for him.

THIS TRANSLATION presents the second version of *Thomas l'obscur* (the only version available at this time). The original work was designated as a novel (*roman*), the revision as a *récit*. Three-quarters of the bulk of the original disappeared in the process.

It is tempting, in this context, to give away some of the secrets of the complex rhetoric of this rich work, to analyse them,* to beg the reader to realize the fact that much of the discomfort he will experience in confronting this work is due to other factors than the translator's failure to iron out difficult points. Suffice it to say that the translator's energies and abilities have been taxed principally to respect and retain the author's level of difficulty, of challenge to the reader, to translate at once the clarity and the opacity of the original.

ROBERT LAMBERTON

* Readers in search of such an analysis are referred to Geoffrey Hartman's perceptive article "Maurice Blanchot: Philosopher-Novelist" in his collection *Beyond Formalism* (Yale University Press, 1970).

Thomas and the Possibility of Translation

Still, one must translate (because one must): at the very least one must begin by searching out in the context of *what* tradition of language, in *what sort* of discourse the invention of a form that is new is situated—a form that is eternally characterized by newness and nevertheless necessarily participates in a relationship of connectedness or of rupture with other manners of speaking. There scholarship intervenes, but it bears less on the nearly unrecoverable and always malleable facts of culture than on the texts themselves, witnesses that do not lie if one decides to remain faithful to them.

L'Entretien infini, 119-120

Blanchot is writing here of the difficulty of approaching the language of Heraclitus. The pretext of his observations on translation is the principle developed by Clémence Ramnoux that Heraclitus' language remains largely untranslatable because of the subsequent formation (completed in the age of Plato and Aristotle) of a basic vocabulary of abstractions that constitute fundamental building blocks of our language and thought.[1] Heraclitus, no less than Homer, speaks a language which is foreign to our own on the levels of vocabulary, of semantic fields, of the relationship of the word to that which it designates.

By the Fourth Century BC we (Europeans) had become linguistic dualists. *Signifiant* and *signifié* were forever divorced, the arbitrariness of their association exposed.[2] Nevertheless, from before the moment of Socrates—in the age which lies in his enormous shadow (since we see him invariably illuminated from a proximal source, himself a myth projected back into the Fifth

119

Century by Plato and Xenophon and constituting the brightness that creates the darkness around and beyond him)—from before Socrates we have a few precious verbal artifacts expressing, manifesting the state of language before the *felix lapsus* of the Greek enlightenment.

Subsequent texts are susceptible to translation. The languages in which they originally became manifest constitute arbitrary wrappings applied to a core of ideas. The situation recalls a science fiction film of the Forties in which substantial, corporeal, but utterly transparent (and therefore invisible) monsters were throwing the world into disorder. Once captured and subdued they revealed their form when coated with *papier mâché*. Any other plastic medium would have served the same expressive function: fly paper, clay, perhaps even spray-paint. These interchangeable media would have expressed the same fortuitously imperceptible outline: the bug eyes, the claws, the saber-toothed-tiger fangs.

The truest Platonist among translators, Thomas Taylor, expressed the relationship with characteristic clarity and good conscience in 1787:

> That words, indeed, are no otherwise valuable than as subservient to things, must surely be acknowledged by every liberal mind, and will alone be disputed by him who has spent the prime of his life, and consumed the vigour of his understanding, in verbal criticisms and grammatical trifles. And, if this is the case, every lover of truth will only study a language for the purpose of procuring the wisdom it contains; and will doubtless wish to make his native language the vehicle of it to others. For, since all truth is eternal, its nature can never be altered by transposition, though, by this means, its dress may be varied, and become less elegant and refined. Perhaps even this inconvenience may be

120

remedied by sedulous cultivation. . . . [*Concerning the Beautiful*, Introduction]

Maurice Blanchot has not, to my knowledge, addressed himself publicly to the problem of translating Maurice Blanchot. I have inevitably wondered what he would think of my efforts, though I have respectfully refrained from entering into a dialogue with him.[3] In the absence of any concrete evidence, I imagine the author of the works of Maurice Blanchot responding to the idea, the fact of the translation of his work (whether mine or another) with that "Nietzschean hilarity" Jeffrey Mehlman sees as characteristic of him—the dialectical twin of the austerity of his prose—and that this imaginary confrontation might be summed up in a phrase from *Celui qui ne m'accompagnait pas* equally evoked by Mehlman: "This gaiety passed into the space I thought I occupied and dispersed me" ("Orphée scripteur," *Poétique* 20 [1974]).

To do justice to the problem of translating Blanchot, to provide a theoretical substructure to lend credibility to the enterprise, would require the formulation of a methodology antithetical to (but not exclusive of) that of Thomas Taylor. This second position would insist upon the absolute opacity of language, on the impossibility of translation, on the incorporeality of the bug-eyed monsters and the absurdity of the effort to reclothe them in some new plastic medium. It would emphasize the integrity of each word, each phrase, each volume of the original text and the necessary triviality of the effort to create some equivalent for it. It would, finally, rush between the legs of the Socratic colossus and take refuge in the absolute refusal of the duality of language, planting itself firmly beyond the fall, beyond the radiance.

121

This methodology would, of course, be no methodology at all. It would not open up a possible mode of action, but humbly, insistently, it would join hands with the viable methodology of Thomas Taylor to undermine and redeem the good conscience of that methodology. On the level of application, it would illuminate (but not solve) the major problem that confronts the translator of Blanchot (and not uniquely of Blanchot: one is tempted to say of any text since Joyce, since Mallarmé, since Nietzsche). This is the problem of the *unit* to be translated. Word, phrase, sentence, paragraph, work: all demand to be rendered as unities, one enclosed within the other without the sacrifice of their integrity. And then there is the bug-eyed monster—Thomas Taylor would call it the eternal thought. Whether or not it exists, it makes its demands, it disrupts the world.

This is the point I have reached in the understanding of my task. Blanchot is not Heraclitus but *Thomas l'Obscur* is more than coincidentally related to Héraclite l'obscur—*ho skoteinos, obscurus,* an epithet used in antiquity to separate *this* Heraclitus from others of the same name, such as the allegorical commentator on Homer. Both epithets are probably developments from *ainiktes,* "the riddler," applied to the Ephesian philosopher by the third-century satirist Timon of Phlius (so Geoffrey Kirk). Blanchot himself insists on the epithet and its force which extends beyond the satirist's trivial slur to indicate the fundamental impulse to "make the obscurity of language respond to the clarity of things" (*L'Entretien infini,* 122). As he goes on to project the heritage of Heraclitus' mode of discourse, expressed in the figure of Socrates himself, Blanchot (as so often in his critical writings) illuminates the method of his own fiction: ". . . Heraclitus then becomes the direct predecessor and as if the first incarnation of the inspired *bavard,* inopportunely and prosaically divine, whose merit, as Plato claims—and surely it is a merit of the first order—consisted in the circularity of his undertakings, which 'by thousands of revolutions and without advancing a step would always return to the same point'" (*L'Entretien infini,* 125). Surely this is the same *bavard* whose austere, gay tone is heard in the belated incarnation of the narrative voice of *Thomas l'obscur.*

What other mysteries does that infuriating title hide? A reviewer of the first edition of this translation pointed to Cocteau's *Thomas l'imposteur* (Naomi Greene in *Novel* 8 [1975]). Perhaps she was correct. While working on the translation I considered every Thomas from the magical evangelist to the master of all the Schoolmen and the unfortunate Archbishop of Canterbury. I find it hard to believe that the second element of the title does not deliberately echo Thomas Hardy's title, and beyond that that the gravedigger scene of the fifth chapter of *Thomas l'obscur* does not echo the arrested burial of Jude's children, and specifically this tableau:

> A man with a shovel in his hands was attempting to earth in the
> common grave of the three children, but his arm was held back by
> an expostultaing woman who stood in the half-filled hole.

But the very ambiguity of the status of these "references" constitutes an element of Blanchot's deliberate smokescreen to foil the efforts of both reader and translator, both condemned to try to determine "in the context of *what* tradition of language, of *what sort* of discourse" his own invention is situated.

The reviewer mentioned above was kind enough to describe

this translaton as "a labor of love." I am deeply grateful to her for that description. For this new edition I have attempted to articulate some of the presuppositions of that labor, from the cooler perspective of eight years' distance. I hope that, in the spirit of Blanchot's essay on Heraclitus, I have remained faithful to *the text itself* and maintained its integrity as a witness.

Robert Lamberton
February, 1981

NOTES

1. These ideas are probably more familiar to English readers in the form they take in the work of Eric Havelock, who explored the problems posed by the language of Homer and the Presocratics in his *Preface to Plato*.
2. The Neoplatonists and the Middle Ages may have forgotten that this was the case, but this quasi-mythic formulation of our intellectual history still retains its basic truth.
3. This is, however, not impossible. Lydia Davis corresponded with Blanchot regarding her beautiful translation of *L'Arrêt de mort* (Station Hill Press, 1978). She has told me that—not surprisingly—he insisted on the importance of her contribution and on the fact that *Death Sentence* was, finally, her book.